Karla Kelsey

Transcendental Factory: For Mina Loy

Winter Editions, 2024

Table of Contents

1905 — *9*

1910 — *17*

1918 — *26*

1931 — *38*

1925 — *51*

1919 — *62*

1965 — *75*

1886 — *85*

1949 — *91*

1936 — *104*

1897 — *118*

Sources — *129*

Acknowledgments — *135*

Perhaps in that transcendental factory in which the "Word" is made "flesh" there is no inertia.

—Mina Loy, *Islands in the Air*

1905

Photographs—

Twenty-three-year-old Mina Loy poses as Mrs. Stephen Haweis, the artist's artistic wife. She sits before an easel wearing a print dress, black belt, and straw hat she's bedecked with enormous rosebuds. The large room is crowded with heavy wood hutches, vases, paintings; and the clutter implies she's in a studio, perhaps Haweis's, near the Luxembourg Gardens where, becoming known for photographs of Auguste Rodin's sculptures, he specializes in gauzy *photographies d'art*. In a rumpled three-piece suit he looks over Loy's shoulder instructing and evaluating the drawing that neither the viewer nor the photographer, Henri Joël Le Savoureux, can see. Her right hand poised in air as if mid-mark, Loy gazes at the camera with a charming smile. Amber broach at her neck, flashing.

Next, Loy's entirely nude, back to the camera in hip-shot pose. Taken by Haweis and titled *Dusie* after the name she's been known by since her art school days in turn-of-the-century Munich. Thigh-length hair swept over her shoulder, her left elbow lifting at an angle, elongating the line of her body. Robe trailing from her hand to pool over the Persian carpet under her feet. Her right knee bent, weight supported by the ball of her foot, her sole dirty or shadowed—it is impossible to tell. A pose similar to Rodin's *Bather* and *Torso of Adèle* and *Toilette of Venus,* cast in bronze.

A third photograph captures Loy from the bust up. She's pinned her paisley-patterned robe to make of her bare chest a white diamond while artfully covering her breasts. She looks in sharp profile to the right, hair Athena-coiled atop her head and tied with a floral scarf. Budapest meets British Empire. Elegant, bohemian, so "Loy (Mlle Mina), née à Hampstead (Àngle-terre). Anglaise"—as she's listed in the catalogue for the 1905 Salon d'Automne above the titles of the four portraits she exhibits. Found on a Weebly site, someone's school project on Loy, with tarot cards and a map of the Arno, this photo is my favorite, but—unattributed and without citation—it might not be of Loy at all.

– o — O — o –

Loy (Mlle Mina), née à Hampstead (Àngle-terre). Anglaise. — 17 rue Campagne Première.

989. — Portrait de Mme Jaffrelot, d.   — now lost
990. — Etude de Tête bretonne, d.   — now lost
991. — Etude de Tête bretonne, d.   — now lost
992. — Etude de Tête bretonne, d.   — now lost

Do Loy's 1905 Salon d'Automne portraits sell? Or when she and Haweis separate the following year, does she give them to Le Savoureux, who will become her lover? Or, the year after, pregnant by Le Savoureux with the child she will name Joella—yet back together with Haweis and moving with him to Florence—cheaper, warmer—does she give her drawings to So-and-So down the street? And if the contents of So-and-So's apartment are left to the rag-pickers after the war, will one of the portraits make its way to the Marché aux Puces—the flea market—and now hang in a stranger's dining room in the South of France?

The frame—walnut inlaid with calla lilies carved in mother-of-pearl.

The first use of the phrases "absinthe spoon" and "Alice blue" are recorded, per the *OED*, in 1905. "Narcissism," in the psychological sense, also enters the lexicon.

– o — O — o –

Mina Loy. Not her birth name Mina Gertrude Lowy, or Löwy, depending on the scholar, on the flourish. Not her married name, Mrs. Stephen Haweis, or her nickname, Dusie, but "Loy"—the name she'd chosen to exhibit under since her first public success as an artist in the 1904 Salon d'Automne. The name under which her first published writing, "Aphorisms on Futurism," will appear in Alfred Stieglitz's journal, *Camera Work,* in 1914.

Photographs of Mina Loy *are* Mina Loy, have become Mina Loy. Glossy black-and-white inserts of Haweis's photos—a touch of Dante Gabriel Rossetti, James McNeill Whistler, and Edward Burne-Jones—are joined by those taken by Man Ray, Berenice Abbott, and Lee Miller in Carolyn Burke's *Becoming Modern: The Life of Mina Loy*, published in hardcover by Farrar, Straus and Giroux in 1996. And then paperback by the University of California Press in 1997. Stacked at the front of bookstores and years later appointed the best place among the remainders, Loy looks out from the cover as she leans toward the small bronze statue she cradles in her left hand, eyes catching Haweis's camera sidelong. A peasant blouse, hair pulled softly back. Also in 1996, *The Lost Lunar Baedeker,* selected poems edited by Roger L. Conover, is published by FSG, and for the first time Loy's poetry reaches a wide audience. Here she poses for Man Ray in profile. A thermometer she's fashioned into an earring dangles from her ear. Eyes closed, she tilts her head toward the light.

In the twenty-first century the cover of *Stories and Essays of Mina Loy* and the second edition of her novel *Insel* use another gauzy Haweis photo—a close-up from the shoulders up, eyes closed again, mouth soft, soft hair pulled softly back in soft disarray. The bottom corner blossoms with light, over-exposed. High-contrast, spectral, she might be one of André Breton's dreamers. Posthumously published.

Sun streams through the vaulted glass roof of the Grand Palais, illuminating homburgs and dark suits. The ladies glide, pastel satin molded over corsets. An occasional loose jewel-tone silk flows from shoulders in the Grecian manner. As they circulate among paintings and statues, a yellow-and-black-striped cape draped *à la Turque* trails through the galleries leaving a wake of Coty's 1905 L'Origan. Carnation, sandalwood, and crushed violets. A bittersweet diamond dust of a perfume. And then entering the Fauve room breathing fierce mauve, Indian yellow, Prussian blue. Water-repellent emerald contours the face of Henri Matisse's *Femme au chapeau*, which Gertrude and Leo Stein purchase and hang in their 27 rue de Fleurus salon.

Loy will return to live again in Paris in 1923. Visiting Stein, whom she'll have known since her Florentine years—1907–1916—Mina will shrug off her floor-length fur and hand it to Alice B. Toklas. A kiss in the air near her cheek. A photo from circa 1908 shows Matisse's *Femme* positioned such that the woman's towering chapeau—more boat or bouquet than hat—leads the eyes to Pablo Picasso's portrait of Stein, directly above. Loy publishes one of the first appreciations of Stein's writing in 1924, and in 1927 presents a lecture in French on Stein's work to an audience of over two hundred gathered at Natalie Clifford Barney's Académie des Femmes.

Loy sketches herself as a stranger. Expression haughty and melancholic. Large eyes dewy and skeptical. Arched eyebrows—her self-proclaimed best feature—full lips, dark hair topped with a flower-bedecked hat. A rough half-moon shape at the breast marks the site of her broach. Silver and amber. Chunks of amber make their way from the Black Sea through the Bosporus Strait to the Sea of Marmara—and from the Sea of Marmara through the Dardanelles to the Aegean. Sand on bare feet, wet hem, gathering amber the size of fists, of hearts, to carve into necklaces, amulets, broaches. Into this broach, within it a wasp suspended, a little sun proliferating bright yellow to sunset warming Oda Janet, born just four months after Loy and Haweis's wedding and dead of meningitis at one year old in May 1905. Oda Janet's violet eyes, a tree weeping resin onto the forest floor.

– o — O — o –

In 1905 Mata Hari, born in the Netherlands as Margaretha Geertruida Zelle, performs her first Javanese-inspired dance at the Musée national des arts asiatiques-Guimet, founded in 1879 by an industrialist to house the artifacts he collected along the Silk Road. Collected, traded, swindled, plundered. Stripping down to her spangles and nude body stocking among statues of dancing

Shiva, Mata Hari is one of Europe's highest-paid dancers. In 1905 the largest diamond ever recorded is found in South Africa. It will subsequently be cut into smaller stones, nine of which will be incorporated into the British royal family's crown jewels. In 1905 the Japanese wolf goes extinct, and in San Francisco a patent is granted for a chainsaw for felling trees. In St. Petersburg the Imperial Guard fires upon demonstrators as they march to the Winter Palace to present the Tsar with a petition for improved working conditions, an end to the Russo-Japanese War, and universal suffrage. In 1905 Max Weber publishes *Die protestantische Ethik und der Geist des Kapitalismus*. Led by W. E. B. Du Bois, a group of Black intellectuals forms the Niagara Movement, forerunner of the National Association for the Advancement of Colored People and Civil Rights Movement. In 1905 Sigmund Freud publishes *Drei Abhandlungen zur Sexualtheorie* exploring psychosexual development. The city of Las Vegas is founded. On Fifth Avenue in New York, Alfred Stieglitz and Edward Steichen open the Little Galleries of the Photo-Secession, later known as 291, and in Trieste James Joyce completes the manuscript of *Dubliners*. The British biologist William Bateson coins the term "genetics" to describe the study of inheritance and variation. In 1905 Upton Sinclair's novel *The Jungle* begins serialization in the American socialist newspaper *Appeal to Reason*, and in London Oscar Wilde's *Salomé*, banned in 1892, has its first UK staging for a private audience at the Bijou Theater. "When I put a green, it is not grass. When I put a blue, it is not the sky," says Matisse, painting at the border between pictorial illusion and pure materiality, and is dubbed a "Fauve," wild beast, along with the other artists exhibiting in Room 7 at the 1905 Salon d'Automne. Picasso ends his Blue Period and begins his Rose Period, and Albert Einstein publishes a paper that explains the photoelectric effect and describes light as quanta, discrete packets of energy. In 1905 Einstein publishes a second paper offering the first experimental proof of the existence of atoms. In 1905 Einstein publishes a third paper outlining the mathematical theory of special relativity. In 1905 Einstein publishes a fourth paper on the energy-mass equivalence, giving the equation $E = mc^2$, and thereafter it is known that energy is mass and mass is energy. It is still 1905.

– o — O — o –

I'm standing in the middle of a crowded gallery telling a friend about my plans for winter in New Haven, Connecticut, reading Loy's unpublished novels at the Beinecke Rare Book & Manuscript Library. "The lampshade-hat poet—loved that biography!" she says. I continue, "Regardless of whether I manage to get them published or not, because of the way her papers are arranged and the fragmentary nature of the manuscripts I need to transcribe them, folder by folder, chapter by chapter, in order to read them." Braids crisscrossed à la Frida Kahlo and fastened with enormous silk roses, my friend takes her phone from her pocket, presses her cheek to my cheek, clicks a photograph of the two of us, and then dives into the crowd. I catch the eye of one of the paintings, a pregnant nude perched on a gold, slipper chair, flying squid circling her otherwise empty room. When the friend's gallery selfie appears on my Instagram feed, my face is blurred, half-out of the frame, the pregnant nude perched atop my friend's crown of braids.

– o — O — o –

Energy is mass and mass is energy. Incandescent skin against the dark backdrop drape. Carpet patterned with botehs and palmettes woven of silk dyed with rose madder, saffron, indigo. Mina's "Aurora" Liberty & Co. robe slips from her hand, her elbow aches in its upward-bent pose.

"The robe's red blossoming chrysanthemums," she says to Stephen as he bends behind his camera, "were inspired by the beauty of imperfection found in hand-carved wooden blocks arranged in a gridded layout to pattern the fabric of a sari. The result: wilderness blooming among dense foliage."

Stephen, standing behind her, breathes on Mina's neck as he arranges her hair.

The composition suggests that after standing and disrobing, her back to the photographer, she will like an Ingres odalisque follow the fall of the fabric to the carpet. And skin soft against bombyx mori and mulberry tree, and near the dye vats were the pig shed and the animals rutting. —*his rosy snout / Rooting erotic garbage* Loy will write in "Songs to Joannes," its first four sections published as "Love Songs" in 1915's inaugural issue of *Others: A Magazine of the New Verse*. Upon its publication, Haweis will tell Loy that she's ruined her reputation.

A palmette spiking emerald in sun, lotus open, silk stretches to breaking as images stream. On the circular end table: suspended in a glass globe, a lobster body topped with the head of a boy, a dumb smile, he's harmless. A figurine. Weightless, he dreams of a girl in a red dress on a swing sailing over the grass. The girl pumping her legs is the lobster boy, is the sun, is shining *palmette palmette*.

Propelled through time by Prussian blue.

Mina in aquarium light, feeling into her lobster body.

1910

In 1910 an uprising against Ottoman rule erupts in Albania, and China bans the institution of slavery, which has existed there since the eighteenth century. The first horror film—a fourteen-minute version of Mary Shelley's *Frankenstein*—is produced by Edison Studios. In 1910 Halley's Comet is visible from Earth and Earth passes through its tail. The comet's next visit I will watch in 1986 from our back porch, eleven years old and bereft of the little chestnut dog who for over a week will have refused food and that day enter the unliving and therefore the stars blur and blur. In 1910 the second meeting of the NAACP is held, the Union of South Africa is created, and the Norwegian Antarctic Expedition departs for the South Pole just as the British Antarctic Expedition departs for the South Pole. In 1910 the Ballets Russes premiers *L'oiseau de feu* in Paris, bringing the Russian composer Igor Stravinsky international fame. A reviewer remarks that the old-gold vermiculation of the production's fantastic backcloth must have been invented from the same formula as the orchestra and dancers. It is in 1910 that Umberto Boccioni, Carlo Carrà, Luigi Russolo, Giacomo Balla, and Gino Severini publish the "Manifesto of Futurist Painters," and Filippo Tommaso Marinetti publishes the Italian version of his novel *Mafarka the Futurist*, a tale of rape, carnage, and Futurist declamation starring an Arabian king with ambitions to conquer all of Africa. In Reno, Nevada, Jack Johnson defeats James J. Jeffries in a heavyweight boxing match, sparking race riots across the United States. Dorothea Tanning, Jacqueline Lamba, Mother Teresa, and Akira Kurosawa are born. Mary Baker Eddy, Leo Tolstoy, and Florence Nightingale die. Simone de Beauvoir is two years old. The last recorded sightings of the yellowfin cutthroat trout and the slender-billed grackle are in 1910. Next year, the gift of an alumnus will establish the Yale Collection of American Literature, which will eventually house the papers of modernists such as H. D., Ezra Pound, William Carlos Williams, Gertrude Stein, Langston Hughes, and Mina Loy. In 1910 Henri Rousseau paints his last completed work, *Le rêve,* depicting Yadwigha, the Polish mistress he loved in his youth posed round and pink and nude on a red velvet divan in the jungle. In 1910 the Japan-Korea Treaty formally annexes the Korean Empire, and the Vatican introduces a compulsory oath against modernism to be taken by all priests upon ordination. In China the Manchurian pneumonic plague begins and by December kills more than forty thousand people. In 1910 the Mexican Revolution begins. In 1910 modern neon lighting is first demonstrated by Georges Claude at the Paris Motor Show. By the year's end Henry Ford has sold ten thousand automobiles.

Loy's daughter Joella is three, her son Giles one. Giulia, the nurse, is efficient and natural at mothering. Haweis begins carrying a pistol and training it on Loy as she walks across the kitchen of the house they've purchased on the Costa San Giorgio with her father's money. Deed drawn up, as was the custom, in Haweis's name. Mabel Dodge, nickname Moose, bursts onto the Florentine scene with her Medici Villa Curonia salon, rose pergola, peacocks strutting the garden, cast-off Parisian dresses, Henri Bergson, Freud, and the New Thought of tarot and spirit readings, Isadora Duncan, Vedanta, Theosophy, and Gertrude Stein. Haweis entertains those who will listen with tales of Mrs. So-and-So who upon his rejection killed herself in the most lurid manner, and then there was Bianca, who had sworn her body to art. After taking her in front of her canvases—discarded. Loy sends her own canvases to galleries but finds, in her twenty-eighth year, dissatisfaction with art, with life, with what she determines is her own utter inability to adjust herself to anything actual because, as she explains in a letter, she has found herself *stirring baby food on spirit lamps,* her best drawings *shoved behind the stove.*

Loy's *Jemima,* thought to be a self-portrait and shown in London at the New English Art Club's 1910 summer exhibition, will be lost. Also from circa 1910, *Ladies at Tea* is lost, *Ladies Watching a Ballet* is lost, *Ladies Fishing* is lost, *Heart Shop* is lost, *The Little Carnival* is lost, *Voyageurs* is lost. Lost, lost—

Although Loy won't publish until 1914, the biography suggests that it is in this caldron that she begins to write.

– o — O — o –

Monday through Friday rain or snow or wind I arrive by 9 a.m. at the Beinecke—a large, marble-clad cube built in the early 1960s by Gordon Bunshaft, who had been catapulted to international fame by his 1952 Lever House, with its sea-green, glass-curtain wall hovering over Park Avenue. The library's thin marble shell is milky white on the outside, but the revolving door leads to an interior bathed in amber. The building's core is a six-story glass tower holding books bound in jewel-toned leather—pig, calf, seal—and in a darkened vitrine John James Audubon's Double Elephant Folio *Birds of America,* open to the Great Egret, waits to have its pages turned. I secure my satchel in a locker and descend to the archive level's marble counter over which the technician passes materials.

The counter is hip-high, ideal for nesting to the body each blue-gray clamshell document box I carry past the security desk to the adjacent reading room. Finished in blonde-woods, the best seats are positioned along the floor-to-ceiling windows looking onto the research level's courtyard. A plantless garden designed by Isamu Noguchi features three large, white marble sculptures. The courtyard is for looking-from-behind-glass-only, so nobody wanders near his pyramid, or his ring-like disk, or his cube balancing on a corner. But even looking-from-behind-glass-only, I feel the marble's porosity, its cold seeping into my body. The pyramid, the disk, the cube.

Mornings I wake to drawn curtains over my sublet's Victorian windows constructing a theater of stained glass. Green-palmette and blue-lotus-print sun pours through, projecting a pattern across the walls as the lazy sounds of New Haven open to the upstairs tenant's TV, the street's idling truck.

The prismatic sun   show
of father's physic bottles
pierced by the light of day

So writes Loy in her verse epic "Anglo-Mongrels and the Rose" from the early 1920s. She writes parallel scenes in two prose manuscripts, *The Child and the Parent,* thought to have been written in Paris in the 1930s, and *Islands in the Air,* written in New York City in the 1940s and '50s.

The archive has six of her seven known autobiographical novels, seemingly all part of the larger sequence, larger cycle Loy called her Book or her novel in letters to Joella and her son-in-law Julien Levy. A suite, a series, a cascade that follows a Loy-like character from childhood and into her teenage years and artistic literary life. She names her alter egos Jemima, Goy, Linda, Sophia, Ova, Mrs. Jones. Roman à clef, autofiction, autotheory, thinly veiled memoir, poet's novel—the majority of the manuscripts are severely fragmented by time, by unfinishing—none of them published until after Loy's death.

The child is carried down the staircase as afternoon sun glitters through glass. She is *riddled with splinters of delight.* Transcribing the passage in the reading room via pencil into my red Clairefontaine, sun angling, sun splintering. And again splintering from notebook to computer at the sublet's dormitory desk. Fingers on the keys. Clack-clack-clack.

– o — O — o –

First shown in Paris at the 1910 Salon des Independents, Rousseau's *Le rêve* is purchased by Ambroise Vollard, noted dealer of French art, who sells it in 1934 to Sidney Janis, an American collector and clothing manufacturer. His fortune was made on the two-pocket short-sleeved shirt. In 1954 Janis sells the *Rêve* to Nelson A. Rockefeller who donates it to the Museum of Modern Art where it currently hangs adjacent to Picasso's 1907 *Les demoiselles d'Avignon* and two self-portraits by Marie Laurencin drawn in pencil and taken from her sketchbooks.

Remembered mainly for her six-year role as Guillaume Apollinaire's muse, Laurencin began studying porcelain painting in Sèvres at age eighteen and continued drawing, painting, and designing until her death, age seventy-three, in 1956. One of the few female Cubists, she exhibited in pioneering Parisian salons, had seven works in the 1913 Armory Show, and appeared in Paris, London, and New York's leading galleries. Sought-after as a society portraitist, Laurencin designed sets and costumes for the Ballets Russes's 1924 production of *Les biches*—a ballet based on a libretto by Jean Cocteau and choreographed by Bronislava Nijinska. Girls in rose drop-waist dresses with tall, feather headdresses, a garçon in a blue velvet leotard, gigolos, a hostess, and a pair of Sapphists. A rumor circulates that Picasso modeled the crouching nude in the lower right-hand corner of *Demoiselles* after Laurencin as tribute to Apollinaire's description of a sex worker who had been dismembered by an explosion, posed à la "open book."

Critiqued for being overly feminine, overly elegant, decorative—a boudoir artist with a pastel palette who painted almost exclusively women, animals, and flowers—Laurencin is also sharp and witty, and parodies the masters. Damasks, centifolias, and gallicas double-distilled to infuse mutton fat. Her 1908 etching *Le Pont de Passy,* for instance, satirizes Édouard Manet's *Luncheon on the Grass*. Laurencin plays the nude, replaces the men with a monkey and a cat.

The empire of self is not stone. Is instead a cloud chamber with water droplets thickening until the interior dissolves into a lake. And sliding through decay on an elongated pink belly. Feeding on decay. And feeding decay with defecation. And the body becomes earth and earth a body, and this is ongoing, inseparable from the notice in the 1910 *Gazette des beaux-arts* of Loy's drawings echoing their titles across time. Inseparable from the largest collection of Laurencin's works, consisting of over six hundred pieces hanging in the now-closed private museum dedicated to her in Tokyo, Japan. Inseparable from the cut-glass box of yellow sugar skulls and *want,* itself a simple syllable which unknowns itself in the saying.

The phrases "picture bride," "data point," and "Oedipus complex" first appear in 1910.

– o — O — o –

Remaining fragments of "Esau Penfold," one of Loy's seven autobiographical novels, tell a story based on Loy and Haweis's relationship through the characters Sophia and Esau. The atmosphere is heavy, slightly sticky. They meet at a Parisian art school, and repulsed by, but pitying him, perhaps slightly fascinated, Sophia lends Esau money and spends increasing time with him at his studio. One night, under the spell of his reading from his manuscript, *some sickly prose from "Digit of the Moon,"* Sophia falls asleep, only to awaken horrified to find herself half-dressed and Esau naked beside her. She has no memory of what has happened but sees *the stricken apparition of a lost virginity slinking along the shadow of the studio wall.*

– o — O — o –

Sick of Stephen holding court from Moose's chaise longue in the little yellow salon—his soiled lace frill, ridiculous satin cape—Mina leaves through the garden, pauses before Isadora who's been standing for hours under the rose pergola with her hands crossed over her solar plexus.

"The sacred self—concealed inside the egg," Isadora says without breaking her pose, "is a soft machine that's part sea creature, one eye edged with the longest of lashes. A single organ, much like a stomach, but a stomach that has turned itself, in turns, inside out and outside in." She is talking to Mina. She is talking to me.

Are they the same, the self and what is said of the self? The self and alternate planes of the self? The self after the dissolution of "I" and "my" and "me"?

I wear Moose's cast-off Poirets with gobs of costume jewelry, heavy boots, masculine hats. I turn away from tea parties and languid ladies to discover the avant-garde's reported degeneracy, anarchism, pornography, which is life blossoming and gasping and burning and burnishing violet, violin, catgut breaking across breaking horsehair strings in the face of bourgeois taste. After all, being conscious consists of remaining with one hand in the realm of possibility penning a dream notebook awake. The airplane and the dragonfly are not released from the hand but from the pen. The closest approximation is an arc of perfect blue becoming a lioness, becoming a flamingo, a blaze of white, a father and daughter dressed in cycling outfits. Enormous flowers replace their human heads: a Gerbera daisy for the father, a poppy for the daughter.

The daughter removes her poppy head and replaces it with a cat's. Persian, Bengal, Siamese, Maine Coon, Russian Blue. The father whispers in the daughter's ear that the other island, the island that cannot be gotten to by train, is the anti-institution of long-sought gestures. On that island in the air one learns with one's body to be both fern and spider, not in aesthetic decadence or just because—look, the body can—but because deity alone makes soft machines dreaming a passageway for a small tribe of magenta-furred primates who began wandering the desert in the Cretaceous period. A ballad sung on a loop.

Running through the oaks and cypresses tearing at my hair, chanting mantra nature utter natal—alarm lament maternal tantalum—tantrum trauma ma tarantula—my bird-eating spider, we had once been so meaty so irrecoverably human—

"She looked like a painting by Augustus John. Her eyes were long and narrow, of a nondescript color, something pale. There was something a little reptilian about her, too. Just as Stephen resembled a lizard or a little tortoise on end, so she made one think of serpents. Lilith her name might have been," Moose will later recall.

– o — O — o –

In the reading room a visiting scholar leans over my shoulder to study my desktop photo of Mina Loy, the one from the Weebly site where she turns in sharp profile to the right, paisley-patterned robe pinned to make a white diamond of her bare chest. "I've seen that floating around," she whispers, "but that's not Loy, you know. It's the silent-film star Evelyn Brent."

– o — O — o –

Back in the city on Saturday, the bells on the hem of my skirt jangle as I climb the stairs to a bar where I take off my coat as I talk to a stranger with a velvet ribbon tied around her neck à la Marie Laurencin. Hanging from both our ears are crystal earrings; in our hands, little glasses of Angostura and soda glinting. I lean close to the stranger who says something about the plunge in temperature which I answer with a story of the pearlescent center of the shell. Its nacre, its iridescence isn't mere decoration but is, rather, a defense against parasites and damaging debris. "Look around," I say, gesturing as if with a cigarette. "We all do this, Marie," I remark to the stranger who is not Marie Laurencin but nevertheless nods, as if this were her name. "Do you not agree that we entomb our potential in a luminous glaze?"

1918

Mina's in the last train car rolling through twilight at December's end, 1917. New York City to San Antonio: 1,800 miles. Solitary, although the train is quite crowded, and the woman next to her is paging through a magazine. Satin-quilted mules, a chiffon handbag, green alligator manicure set and matching passport case. At the border Mina takes her seat in an armored car for eight hundred more miles past mines of silver, opal, crystal, amethyst to Mexico City. A touch of metal on the tongue, sand in the throat. Gold vibrates before the snowy peaks of Popocatépetl and Iztaccíhuatl—volcanic lovers.

The Aztec princess Iztaccíhuatl had been promised in marriage to the warrior Popocatépetl upon his victory in battle. Coral wrapped around her wrists. But before he returns, a jealous suitor tells her that Popocatépetl has died, declares the beloved's soul a hummingbird following the sun. Grief-stricken, Iztaccíhuatl's body contracts, shatters opals from rock. Returning in glory only to find his betrothed prepared for burial, Popocatépetl piles ten hills together, constructs a tomb close to the sun. Carrying her body to the summit he kneels before her with a torch, shaking and smoking steam and fire and ash.

The same violet sky, soft ash sky, hovered above Spanish conquistadors led by Pedro de Alvarado as they killed thousands of Aztecs during a ceremonial dance. And the Spaniards spreading the European disease: a Franciscan monk notes the impossibility of burying the dead, too many, and so pulling their houses down around them.

Light rain, and the train pulls into Mexico City's Terminal Buenavista where Arthur Cravan, a.k.a. Colossus—poet, proto-Dadaist, pugilist, draft-dodger, and Oscar Wilde's nephew, no less—has been waiting.

As she descends from the train car, silver and marigold fill Mina's nose, push into her mouth.

Onto the streets of Mexico City she steps with a hummingbird necklace nipping at her neck.

– o — O — o –

Loy arrives in Mexico City in time for the new year, marries Cravan in January 1918, is pregnant by July, and by November arrives alone in Buenos Aires via Valparaíso and a Japanese hospital boat. Upon her arrival: news of the ceasefire between the Allies and Germany. In fall of 1918, Cravan, who doesn't have the papers necessary for official travel, will repair a small boat and set sail from Salina Cruz. Although he's supposed to meet Loy in Buenos Aires, he's never heard from again.

– o — O — o –

There are no known photographs of Loy in Mexico City. No record of drawings or writing she might have done there, but one of my favorite photos is taken the spring before she leaves. It is May 1917, and she's lived in New York City since the previous October—ten-year-old Joella and eight-year-old Gilles staying in Florence under the care of the headmistress of their school. *Others* has just devoted the entirety of Volume 3, Number 6, price 15 cents, to her scandalous "Songs to Joannes," and Loy is caught mid-gesture turning toward the camera, her arms extended, hands flexed as if dancing. She wears a white coat part Pierrot, part galleon's captain. Her face uplifted, expression strong but indefinable. Long silver earrings dangle from her ears. In the background are her studio and the only known photographic evidence of the lampshades she made and sold in New York. Three of the four shades with their tapered empire shape decorated with polka-dots, stripes, and scallops could be found today in Target, Anthropologie—on Amazon. The fourth, rectangular with rounded edges, features knots of flowers—neo-Victorian.

Dressed for The Blind Man's Ball—"The dance will not end till the dawn. . . . Romantic rags requested," as advertised in the second and final issue of *The Blind Man,* the little magazine put together by Marcel Duchamp, Beatrice Wood, and Henri-Pierre Roché. Four of its fifteen pages are by Loy, and the issue centers around a defense of Mr. Richard Mutt's *Fountain*—the Buddha of the Bathroom—suppressed from April's Society of Independent Artists show where Loy exhibited *Making Lampshades* alongside Wood's *Un peut (peu) d'eau dans du savon*. A headless nude with a bar of soap affixed over her sex, men leave calling cards tucked into the painting's frame.

The Blind Man opens with Stieglitz's black-and-white photo of *Fountain*, raised on a plinth and backed by a Marsden Hartley. The last spread is "compiled by Mina Loy," titled "O Marcel—otherwise I Also Have Been to Louise's," a fractured textual collage of seemingly overheard gossipy snippets. A simultaneous impression presented in typewriter font—*I don't like a lady in evening dress* and *I want some cigarettes for Mina* and *You speak like Carlo* and *There's always a sky in heaven* and *My ancestor is tall people*—

For Mexico City with Cravan, Loy leaves nightly gatherings at Walter and Louise Arensberg's apartment at 33 West 67th where she talks until dawn with Duchamp, Gabi Picabia, Berenice Abbott, and Man Ray. Dab Chypre behind the ears, at the wrists, to enter a room with African orange flower, Amalfi lemon, carnation, musk. For Mexico City, Loy leaves her reputation: not only a great beauty but a provocative poet whose writing and illustrations have appeared almost exclusively in American avant-garde magazines—*Camera Work*, *Trend*, *Rogue*, *Others*, *The Blind Man*. Profiled as the quintessential modern woman in *The Evening Sun*, a poet and painter traversing language and nation to talk Futurism, Gertrude Stein, and free verse in English, French, Italian, and German. Leaves acting with William Carlos Williams in the Provincetown Players' avant-garde plays. Leaves a community of artists expansive enough to embrace even Elsa von Freytag-Loringhoven, the Baroness, who shaves her head and paints it vermillion, wears teaspoon earrings, a taillight bustle on her dress, her 1918 sculpture *Limbswish* a curtain tassel and metal spring attached to her belt, and in 1917 she turns a cast-iron plumbing trap upside down on a wood miter box, titling it *God*. And if *God* wasn't phallic enough, casting an enormous phallus in plaster, carrying it like an infant, presenting it to unsuspecting women on the street. One image is lost, another circulates. In 1982 Robert Mapplethorpe will photograph Louise Bourgeois wearing a tufted monkey-fur coat with her own phallic 1968 sculpture *Fillette* tucked under her right arm.

What kind of life might Loy have made if she stayed? Observe the Baroness. By 1917 she's a war widow, and at the age of forty-two lives in a small apartment in the Lincoln Arcade Building on Broadway—forty dollars a month, home and studio to artists until cleared out: demolished in the 1960s for the Lincoln Center for the Performing Arts and the Juilliard School. Play a little Satie, a little Stockhausen. Here Duchamp also lives, and he and the Baroness meet for late-night excursions across the city gathering discarded strips of celluloid, tin cans, toys, vegetables, iron, stamps, pins. Unable to make rent, the Baroness sets out for Philadelphia, offering her services as artist's model. Entering the painter George Biddle's studio she sweeps off her scarlet raincoat to stand entirely nude except for one arm covered shoulder to wrist with celluloid curtain rings stolen from Wanamaker's. Over each breast a tin tomato can fastened together with green string. Between the tomato cans hangs a canary in a miniature cage. Biddle, the Baroness is to write, although quite rich, insists on bargaining over the price—"You all had money-safety but nobody paid me a decent price for the show he enjoyed." She's soon back in New York, supported by Abbott and then Djuna Barnes, whose own finances are perennially precarious. By 1923 the Baroness returns to Berlin, selling newspapers on street corners. She spends the last year of her life in Paris where at the age of fifty-three she dies of gas asphyxiation.

– o — O — o –

To disappear, as Haytham el-Wardany instructs in his little blue book titled *How to Disappear*, sit in a public place and tune in to the sounds around you. Observe not only the words of a conversation but their textures. Become so entirely absorbed in those sounds that your thoughts, your self, your language melt away.

– o — O — o –

Loy, nearly thirty-five years old, leaves New York and the financial security—or what in her life of insecurity will pass for security—of her modestly successful lampshade business. Leaves her apartment on West 57th not far from the Arensbergs, and on my way home from Central Park I look up at the Steinway Tower, wondering if her building was replaced by this skyscraper, one of the tallest in the US and among the thinnest in the world.

Ear of corn, sickle, and bandolier. Mexico City, 1917, is not the post-revolution community of national and international modernist intelligentsia it will become in the '20s with the likes of Edward Weston and Tina Modotti with their rooftop azotea fitted out with a woven rug, a few old chairs, a writing desk, and a view of Mexico City's cupolas. Is not the refuge it will become in the '40s for Leonora Carrington, Remedios Varo, and Kati Horna, fleeing the Second World War. In 1917 Mexico City is ravaged by poverty and civil war. Sickle, bandolier, and guitar. There, apart from Cravan, Loy knows only Bob Brown from the West Village who has holed up with his fellow ex-pat bohemians in an ancient hidalgo mansion a far cry from the Arensbergs' duplex with its Matisses, Picabias, Brâncuşis, African and pre-Columbian art.

The question of why Loy would leave New York inspires speculation over the intoxicating effect of Cravan despite—or perhaps because of—his untamed nature, picking fights, insulting people, collecting and discarding women. Loy had known him less than nine months, but already he was expensive Siamese kittens, old leather, a cockfight feather—torn and bloody. Added to this: four days prior to the April 10 opening of the Society of Independent Artists exhibition, the US declares war on Germany. That summer Congress passes the Espionage Act, and as of June 15 any dissenter could be, like Emma Goldman, charged with treason, fines, deportation. *The Blind Man* is published solely under Wood's name to protect Roché and Duchamp from deportation, and the editors distribute the issue by hand. The Arensberg circle disperses, Stieglitz closes his gallery, the Baroness, arrested as a spy, is imprisoned for three weeks in Connecticut. Loy's divorce from Haweis is finalized, she's granted custody of her children, and she's allowed to resume her maiden name. She receives news of her father's death and her subsequent small inheritance. And so, go to Mexico? What did Loy, artist, writer, immigrant, half-Jew, just-above-the-poverty-class-by-the-skin-of-her-teeth have to lose?

$$- o — O — o -$$

Loy's archive includes typescript manuscripts and hand-scrawled notes on brittle browned paper and letterhead from the lamp shop she had established in Paris. Patent designs for toys, corsets, and window-washing devices. Sketches of faces, of dresses, of cats. Alice Toklas could decipher Stein's undecipherable handwriting and typed, edited, and organized her manuscripts. Loy's handwriting is relatively neat—not much slant, closed loops. Strong crossbars and dotted i's. I suspect Joella typed some of Loy's drafts, but more likely Loy and a few unrecorded typists alone did this. A section-break marker she creates sometimes by hand—looping ribbons of o's with delicate dashes, string of gems—and sometimes by typewriter—interconnects projects, forms constellations across the dark.

$$- o — O — o -$$

$$- o — O — o -$$

$$- o — O — o - o — o —$$

The manuscript for her unpublished "Colossus" is held in a private collection, but if it is a full draft, or fragments, or unfinished, and whether it is the only draft—nobody says or nobody knows, although excerpts appear in *New York Dada,* in 1986. The trace in Loy's archive is only a few crossed-out pages, drafts of other manuscripts written on the back. Two hand-written sheets are housed in the Beinecke's Carolyn Burke Collection on Mina Loy and Lee Miller. One page is on lined notebook paper, written in French, numbered at the top. The words *Cravan* and *Colossus* in a loose, large hand. The other, unlined, has rips along the left margin as if it had been kept in a notebook. Written in English, a small hand, the page features a character named *the woman* and another named *Colossus.*

After the woman and Colossus marry they settle in a tenement room—shared courtyard, kitchen, bathroom—near the Basilica of Santa María de Guadalupe. The woman does the washing, makes tortillas on the communal stove, and tends to Colossus when he falls grievously ill. Low on money, at times they eat only every other day, flavor coffee grounds with orange rinds. The woman looks after Colossus with more devotion than he has ever lavished on the green stockings of a countess in New York, where he—or, rather, where Cravan—played the salon game—according to William Carlos Williams's *Autobiography*—of tracing the countess's legs for hours.

"Pregnant on the shore," Williams will write, Loy "watched the small ship move steadily away into the distance."

But pregnant with her fourth child, Fabi, Loy had already boarded a Japanese hospital ship bound for Valparaíso on the way to Buenos Aires, where before hearing of Colossus's disappearance she learned the Great War had ended.

The scent of stone and excreta overpower the marigold, the coconut grove, the tobacco, the chili. Of Colossus, Loy writes: *He could push his entire consciousness into a wisp of grass.*

Colossus—

—cool, locus, loco, cuss, sus, sou, solo, soul, loss, lo, o, so, sos, sos, sos, sos, sos—

Throughout the 1920s and 1930s the avant-garde salons of Paris and New York buzz with speculation, ongoing to this day: Had Cravan, upon disappearing in 1918, actually died? Or, bored of domesticity and Loy now pregnant, had he run off with her money, which he had kept for them carefully tucked in a leather billfold? And what of his other women? Someone will insist they've seen Cravan now manifest as this or that tramp, this or that counterfeiter, con artist, because, after all, he was much more those things than father material. Loy will speculate that he was murdered, inquiring at the British Secret Service and US State Department, who had found him of sufficient interest to keep a file: draft dodger, petty miscreant, once made Leon Trotsky's acquaintance aboard a ship. Colossus's lungs fill with water. Colossus sails to Puerto Vallarta to meet his lover. A switchblade cuts his throat. A prison guard laughs as he places food just out of reach.

- o — O — o -

Leonora Carrington plays a woman veiled in black and carrying an umbrella in Kati Horna's photograph series, *Oda a la Necrofilia,* Mexico City, 1962. Photo by photo she traverses a small white room filled with a white bed, pillows supporting a white oval death mask. White light falls through French doors. Undressing, the figure pauses beneath her open umbrella to smoke a cigarette, her reflection casting back the polished image of a film star. The mask watches in each shot. By the end of the series Carrington sits naked on the bed, forehead bowed to mattress. Back to the camera, her vertebrae and ribs extend into the ripples of the sheets.

In 1918 Fabian Avenarius Lloyd a.k.a. Arthur Cravan a.k.a. Colossus drowns or is murdered or sails away or counterfeits himself a new identity. In 1918 the Spanish Flu is first observed in the US in Haskell County, Kansas; by October it courses across Mexico. In 1918 Maria and Julian Martinez revive the technique for black-on-black pottery, basing their designs on shards found on an ancestral Pueblo site. In the 1918 Battle of Bear Valley US troops engage Yaqui Indian warriors in one of the last battles of the American Indian Wars. In 1918 the Russian Red Army is formed, and in the UK propertied women over the age of thirty are given the vote. On March 6 the US Navy tests the first drone. In 1918 the Carolina parakeet goes extinct, Russia withdraws from World War I, the Spanish Flu becomes a pandemic and in its second wave the sick turn blue, their lungs fill with fluid, and they die within hours or days of developing the first symptoms. In 1918 German U-boats appear in US waters, and the Romanov family is executed by order of the Bolshevik party. In 1918 World War I ends. Roughly one thousand pilot whales strand in the Chatham Islands.

– o — O — o –

Grief-stricken, Iztaccíhuatl lies silent and cold. Paving stones and gravel are sharp through Mina's gold-painted ballet slippers, passing the shady entrances to churches with their flickering votives. She's passing market stalls of white linen embroidered with exquisite bestiaries, geometries, gardens. Passing children playing in the streets, passing Casa Azul where in 1918 ten-year-old Frida Kahlo is a flick of black braids, a yellow dress in a tree. Colossus gives Mina their last centavos to feed a starving dog.

I walk the neighborhood with a bag of stinking meat until twilight to look for the dog, his outsized skull, his chestnut body. He is not to be found, and other, stronger dogs fight for the meat. It is one hundred years in the future, and I by my own first husband am pushed face down on the bed in a luxury honeymoon hotel not far from this impoverished Mexican street. A raw splitting from anus to brainstem, claws digging the down bedcover, and from then on the sky had a streak of blood in it, regardless of the many sugar skulls offered up to the tarantula in her glass cage. As this happens and re-happens the dogs fight for the prize of meat, and it is still 1907, and Haweis still trains his pistol upon Loy as she walks across the room.

I watch the horizon, and sand pours from my body. I watch the horizon, and Colossus pours through a hole at the top of my head, slides a slow liquid gold through my chest cavity to settle in my womb. On the fortieth night I on the shore strip myself of dress, flesh, give myself over to salt and wave and wind until I am overcome by the image of a woman in a blue tunic decorated with woven flowers formed of feathers and little bits of gold. She wears gold disks in her ears and in her nose a gold ornament which hangs over her mouth. She is crowned with a garland of red leather woven like a braid, and from its sides emerge splendid green feather ornaments that look like horns. She touches my forehead, lips, belly as dawn slashes the clouds with unnatural orange.

Bending to meet my eyes in the mirror, Mina fastens a red coral necklace around my neck, and I ask her if she made peace with not knowing what had happened to Cravan. Or at least with the idea that he might have abandoned her, shed his identity. Wanting him to be alive no matter what, but also not wanting to have been left by her greatest love. No matter what. As if in response Mina says she's recently read that neuroimaging suggests that careful contemplation of surrealist images helps people to process death. "O infinite passageways to the unliving, to the fourth dimension, the infrathin."

1931

Mina steps with the quietude of Paris 1931 before dawn to walk ten minutes home down rue du Cherche-Midi from Constantin Brâncuși's Impasse Ronsin atelier. Commanding the self to unruffle the mind and listen to the sparrows. To what day says prior to delivery trucks and cafés setting out tables. Constantin just now in Mina's absence scooping tea leaves from his kettle, polish of metal, jagged rough marble. "Constantin," Mina said upon leaving, "we must never forget your name means 'steadfast' and was shared with eleven Roman and Byzantine emperors, several Bulgarian emperors, and two Greek kings." Constantin who smells of stone, horse, rotted plum.

They talked all night. How to keep the body loose within tightening economy? Architecture within architecture within architecture.

Brâncuși since 1910 has created new works not as individual pieces but as components of mobile groups clustered throughout his studio. He often explains this, as if forgetting that for nearly a decade Mina has regularly frequented his atelier, has many times sat, just so, on a chair between a marble block and the stove. Has turned her face to the heat. Oval, sphere, angle, cube. Form's completion disrupted by notch, furrow, cleft.

A layer of space. A circumference that properly belongs to the body though invisible to the eye. How else drive a car, ride a horse? A leaf placed on a piece of film set on an electromagnetic plate reveals that the plant's aura spikes electric violet. Extension, network, constellation, fourth dimension. If the event is Mina, then surrounding the event is the invisible fact that "Mina" means "with gilded helmet." White silk dress. Perfume of roses. Means also "of the sea." Also: "will," "desire," "protection." And, in Persian: "azure," "blue glass gem," "enamel." In Coptic Egyptian, like Constantine: "steadfast."

Also around each body, entity, name—a circumference of time. Brâncuși's *L'orgueil*, head of a girl cast in bronze, shared the 1906 Salon d'Automne with Loy's *L'amour dorloté par les belles dames*. Five water-colored women in pastel flounces and shawls pose surrounding a fainting nude figure with delicate wings. It's easy to miss Eros's genitalia, so finely drawn, but once noticed the expressions on the women's faces shift from sisterly interest to irreverence and delight. Except for the woman in pink, who sits facing the viewer, her back to the scene. She's slightly bored as she leans on an enormous blue medallion intaglioed with peacocks and vines.

The closeness of roses. Mina breathes them in as she makes her way down the boulevard in her rose mask.

– o — O — o –

To hold in the mouth the halo of space surrounding each syllable because the body and the life, the life and the body are part of the gall gates of the house. The roof beams, the walking sticks, the distaffs, the spoons. Breathing in on the contraction to a count of four. Exhaling for a count of six on the release. Repeat. Even while walking across the café, across the square, across the stage in the dark. Repeat this moving through water. These gestures confect a process that speeds up until they go unnoticed. But slow them down, film on a reel, they become offerings. The horse in mid-gallop floats all his legs in the air.

– o — O — o –

In 1931 drought overtakes the midwestern plains of the US, and dust from overworked land billows into storms. Scientists at Columbia University demonstrate the existence of heavy water, an essential step in transforming common uranium into the plutonium that will fuel nuclear bombs. In 1931 László Bíró first exhibits his ballpoint pen in Budapest. Nylon is invented. The Empire State Building is completed and opens as the tallest building in the world. Charlie Chaplin's *City Lights* premieres. *Dracula* starring Bela Lugosi premieres. *Frankenstein* starring Boris Karloff premieres. In 1931 Boris Yeltsin, James Dean, Rupert Murdoch, and Desmond Tutu are born. US unemployment reaches eight million. In 1931, the Black American teenagers Willie Roberson, Olen Montgomery, Ozie Powell, Eugene Williams, Roy Wright, Clarence Norris, Andy Wright, Charlie Weems, and Haywood Patterson are wrongly accused of raping two white women aboard a Southern Railroad freight train in northern Alabama. All but the thirteen-year-old Roy Wright, a minor, are sentenced to death. Virginia Woolf's *The Waves,* Pearl S. Buck's *The Good Earth,* and John Steinbeck's *The Grapes of Wrath* are published. Bunker's woodrat goes extinct. In 1931 seven to nine million people visit the Colonial Exposition in Paris. The first Surrealist exhibition in the US opens at the Wadsworth Atheneum in Hartford, Connecticut, before moving on to Julien Levy's gallery in New York City. Salvador Dalí paints *The Persistence of Memory*. Frida Kahlo paints *Frida and Diego Rivera.* Georgia O'Keeffe paints *Cow's Skull: Red, White, and Blue.* The George Washington Bridge opens, and the Whitney Museum of Art is founded. The electric razor and the aerosol can are invented. In 1931 Greta Garbo stars in MGM's *Mata Hari*. Gowns by Adrian include a fifty-pound gold mesh beaded dress with dolman sleeves inspired by Léon Bakst's costumes for the Ballets Russes. In 1931 fashionable accessories are suede gloves with matching bag and shoes, a red or gray fox fur flung over one shoulder, batik scarves, large rings, and watches set with gems. In 1931 an average of 133 businesses collapse each day. Premier banks in Austria and Germany become insolvent, and the US suffers a second round of bank failures. In 1931 Thomas Edison, Anna Pavlova, and Khalil Gibran die. On May 4, speaking in private to Nazi party members, Hitler says, "We can achieve something only by fanaticism." "The Star-Spangled Banner" becomes the US national anthem. In 1931 Al Capone is indicted for tax evasion, a British committee awards sole ownership of the Wailing Wall to Muslims, and Amelia Earhart crashes in Abilene, Kansas, exiting the fiery remains of the plane unscathed.

– o — O — o –

For mid-mornings at Le Dôme, Mina selects a table by its relation to other tables. Her preferred place: outside, next to the potted majesty palm. She and the palm eavesdrop in English, French, German, and Italian; with her little gold pen she begins to write the next section of her Book. It is June 15, 1931, a Monday under the sign of Gemini's incompleteness. Mina once had been a sphere, now is hewn in two. Why else pause over coffee, over a cradle, over a sewing machine, over a ledger, over a telegraph, over the writing of a book while caught in the sensation of loss? Lost in that primordial divorce, divide, disunion, uncoupling, unyoking. Oh, why do we ever part, cut, detach, break, burst, sever, and scatter?

At the next table a woman recently arrived from New York City spoons sugar into her tea as she tells her companion about the premiere of Martha Graham's *Lamentation*, which she attended at Maxine Elliott's Theater on Broadway.

As the four-minute dance begins, Graham sits spot-lit on a spare bench. Statuesque, wrapped head to toe in a tube-like costume of violet jersey, legs turned out, knees out in a wide second. A birthing position. The violet jersey is attic drapery, a shroud stitched from Chanel couture twisting as the dancer's torso angles, pelvis rooted and torso reaching. The costume clings, stretches with the extension of arms, head, legs. The spiral begins from the inside of the body and works its way out. Wrapped in mood, light falls on Graham's lifted face as she contracts and releases a form of grief that doesn't drop like a flower or attitudinize like a frieze but spirals from the center through torso and arms. A star falls into itself then bursts out.

What had been *I* reveals I had been all along not only eternal light but sparrow, shoe, tooth, teacup, chewing gum, vowel.

The arm a wing. The wing an arm.

The brass sphere rocks back and forth. On vacation at the shore waking early and pulling on her lover's nearly dress-length sweater and pinning it here and here and here before making her way to the water, Gabrielle Chanel discovers that the raw jersey fabric of men's underwear and sailor sweaters neatly tailors to the female form.

"The scandal of it;" says the woman's Parisian companion—*la danse*, while seated—"only an American could dream such a thing." Sparrows skitter after crumbs of a baguette. The dance invites the dead to appear for a moment in the theater, a feather drifting down as the houselights are raised. A feather resting in the hand. A feather tucked into a pocketbook.

Lamentation.

—aeolian alien anima anneal annotate atilt atman atone elm elation eon entail entoil eolian inane inmate innate intent into iota intone lament lamina latent alone—

At my café table I am writing this down while saying "yes" to the waiter and his suggestion of another espresso, as if all I had on my mind was espresso. "Yes" to the square of lemon cake sent over with the compliments of the man at table five, as if all I had in mind was the man at table five. Meanwhile, I say to myself, for wine glass write "breakage." For progression of society write "knot." Between each phrase write the telegraphic "stop."

– o — O — o –

A gramophone sings. An airplane roars. For the 1931 Paris Colonial Exposition, open since May, the French milliner Agnès has designed an Algerian hat with a fetching "native" side point. Woven of strips of brown wool to show hair at one side in the smart new manner, this hat is worn by none other than that icon of style, Baba. Since prior to the exhibit's opening, Knox in New York has had this hat.

New York possesses the hat, sells the hat. Paris replicates the colonies: within fifteen minutes of the Palais Garnier visitors are transplanted to the Bois de Vincennes—exhibition grounds populated by the jungles of Africa, palaces of Angkor, entire villages of Congo huts, Chinese temples, and, as if in collusion with Knox in New York the buildings of Mount Vernon, manufactured by Sears, Roebuck and Company. The exhibition doesn't include the property's eight thousand acres divided into five farms, which had been worked by over five hundred enslaved people at any given time. The Guyanese exhibit offers instead butterflies of blue enamel. Fine hammocks.

The pavilions have been created for Baba entering through the Port d'Honneur in a smart tweed suit. Baba in baby blue with navy bows at the neck, shoulders, hips, and wrists posing with an enormous plume of cotton candy before the oval lawn parterre. Baba languid in silver Vionnet bias-cut silk against the central obelisk. Baba slinking past twenty-two illuminated pyramids. Baba in black with a necklace featuring an enormous zircon cross pausing before the performance of cascades and jets colored by electric lights in the "Theater of Water." In 1931 "supermarket," "nuclear physics," and "military-industrial complex" enter the lexicon.

L'intransigeant and *Paris-soir* report that in thrall to the Colonial exposition numerous designers and shop owners have replaced the traditional white wax mannequin with dark-gold abstracted figures by Siegel and Stockman, makers of tailors' dummies, window bust forms, and mannequins since 1867. Their heads bear a striking resemblance to Brâncuși's 1909 *La muse endormie,* just as their limbs resemble his 1923 *Bird in Space.* These golden goddesses pause languidly in the arched windows of the high, pink Madagascar Palace, crowned by four bull heads. They linger seductively in the French national pavilion wearing lingerie, or draped in Mme Pangon textiles—velvet, chiffon, and silk batik printed with soap bubbles, peacock feathers, seaweed, fruit.

Once an ancient forest home to boar, deer, ortolan. Bacchus, Diana, Silvanus. Then the hunting ground of royals. Then military training grounds. Then public park, then prison grounds housing Denis Diderot and the Marquis de Sade. Mata Hari during the First World War prior to her execution in the Bois de Vincennes blows a kiss to the firing squad.

On the opposite side of the exhibition's "Theater of Water" stands Giles, back from the dead. Stolen from Florence when he was twelve by Haweis who, while Loy was in New York, had taken him to live in the Caribbean. Giles died unexpectedly two years later, in 1923. Yet here he is, grown into his safari jacket and pith helmet. By the time the waters stop, he's vanished.

"If you see Mina," Haweis had written, "tell her that he lived finely and died bravely"—making much of the fact that Loy had left Giles's letters unanswered. If her silence and not a rare cancer hadn't killed him, it at least amplified, Haweis wrote, Giles's suffering. Had Loy really left her son's letters unanswered—had she, and why?

"At the Exposition," a critic writes, "we reconstitute the marvelous stairway of Angkor Watt and make the sacred dancers twirl, but in Indochina we shoot, we deport, we imprison."

On the fringes of the Bois where itinerants pitch their tents, Mina joins a stranger at his campfire. Staring into flames she states Giles's death was the most difficult thing. And then repeats "the most difficult thing" with gestures. She puts her hands in the fire, and I put my hands in the fire, fire travelling up my sleeves, down my dress. The stench of burnt cotton, burnt hair, burnt skin.

A radio broadcast cuts out after reporting that Britain has just released Mahatma Gandhi from prison, where he'd been held for walking twenty-four days to the Arabian Sea to lead an illegal harvest of salt from its waters in protest of the British salt tax. When the broadcast cuts back in a reporter announces that between March 2020 and November 2021 the collective wealth of the world's richest increased by 1.3 billion dollars a day. Dresses made from the loveliest iridescent fabric lift, all at once, into flame.

– o — O — o –

I go to the library always alone. Alone with soft lights creating the halo of space in which I sit, documented by security cameras and therefore inhabiting the quintessential position of the twenty-first century. Always alone but never alone. Loy in an unadorned peasant dress, pearls, and chandelier earrings, hair parted in the middle and pulled softly back, sits in the center with Berenice Abbott—Brâncuși and Tristan Tzara to their right, Jane Heap and Margaret Anderson to their left. Empty wine glasses in the foreground, the group casts shadows across the crumbling walls of Brâncuși's atelier in this file folder's copy of a 1923 photograph. An orb of light nestles in Loy's lap just where his *Sleeping Muse* might have been.

The next folder's manuscript, nearly one hundred years old, disintegrates along the edges. Where will Loy be found when she leaves her paper form? Typescripts, handwritten drafts, doodles, drawings, patent designs unfold across whatever is at hand: address books, cablegrams, tracing paper, notebooks, typewriter paper, invoice slips. Letterhead from the Paris lamp shop partially funded by Peggy Guggenheim, opened in 1926 and sold in 1930. The shop's address is printed in peacock blue. The lamps had been a success but overwhelming, especially after Julien Levy came calling. Tobacco, vetiver, and something indistinguishable but quite sharp. Young Julien admiring Loy, flirting with Joella then marrying her six months later. They depart for New York in 1928. Nine-year-old Fabi tending her menagerie.

Mina Loy
Rue du Colisée, 52
Paris
Téléphon : Élysées 19–95
R.C. Seine No 359.000

Who would answer if I dialed the shop's number? Digitized, does Loy live in the space between paper and screen? She made her lampshades from fragile material—cellophane, paper, the new mailable plastics.

Brâncuși in contrast ensures the preservation not only of his works but also of the spatial configuration so essential to his practice by bequeathing his original studio to the French state upon his death in 1956. Workbench and tools exactly as he left them along with 137 sculptures, 87 bases, 41 drawings, 2 paintings, and over 1,600 glass photographic plates and original prints. The studio is dismantled and then reconstructed at the Centre Pompidou inside a building designed by Renzo Piano in 1977.

Joella donated Loy's papers to the Beinecke in 1974 and 1975. A collection of 4.25 linear feet housed in 8 boxes. Compare this with the H. D. Papers: 30.88 linear feet, 71 boxes. The Gertrude Stein and Alice B. Toklas Papers: 93 linear feet, 173 boxes, which is joined by the Gertrude Stein and Alice B. Toklas Collection: 24.41 linear feet, 45 boxes. The Ezra Pound Papers: 203.4 linear feet, 300 boxes. The Langston Hughes Papers: 305 linear feet, 673 boxes.

Loy's most brittle pages are preserved by clear, polyester protective sleeves, a material perhaps not unlike Verrovoile, the delicate plastic—*glass fabric*—Loy invented for the detailed work of her sculptural floral lamps, their finely lined leaves. Arum lily. Trumpet lily. Lamp shop stationery torn at the corner, Loy worries her designs are being stolen, and I am so close to knowing the light or heavy fabric of her dress and Clarice Lispector–like in the living room balancing a typewriter on her knees. Fountain pen, ballpoint pen, biro, pencil, and red crayon. Incomplete.

The body is us, exceeds us.

Only Joella, Fabi, Julien, Djuna Barnes, and Natalie Clifford Barney knew of Loy's novel, her prose, her Book. A curator suggested I read Loy's letters and drafts housed in the papers of Carl Van Vechten—the writer and photographer who acted as informal literary agent for Hughes, Wallace Stevens, and Stein and promoted the Harlem Renaissance to white audiences. He and Loy became intimate friends after meeting at Moose's Villa Curonia salon in 1913, and Van Vechten was essential in placing Loy's early work. In a 1915 letter she describes a new project that must have been a novel, *the book goes well—26 thousand words so far—I think it is new—I wonder if it will get published—of course it is <u>entirely imaginary</u>!* In June she had written him with excitement about what seems to have been the same project: *I am writing a book—the purest—most truthful—and personally imaginative book that could be written*—She goes on to offer a bit of the book about the Colosseum at night, filling an entire stationery page with a sensual encounter with *stamens of flowers . . . the spring beating things into her arms which would not come.*

Box 6 holds shorter works—stories, essays, plays, meditations and uncategorizable writings mostly unpublished until the scholar Sara Crangle transcribes and edits them for the 2011 *Stories and Essays of Mina Loy*. "Mi & Lo," sixty pages of philosophical fragments on form, universal energy, and the body as a lightning rod, commands attention. Undated but thought to have been written in Paris in the early '30s, the first page is just seven words scrawled in cursive, letters spaced equally, continuous but with more pressure on downward strokes and crossbars—

Power
  force animating
  Body –
    Electric Prayer
      <u>*etc*</u>

I rush across this page, hardly notice it in the reading room, but at the sublet I zoom in on the digitized version to study the word *Power*. Nearly crayon-like when compared with the smooth graphite of Loy's other lettering. Perhaps written in a pastel pencil she had just been drawing with. This, and its cramped placement on the page, creates the impression she added it after the fact. Or perhaps it was written first and after meditating on *Power* Loy expanded into *force animating*. The solar plexus's little sun. Paper and pencil reveal the hand, reveal the temporal nature of all the writer touches—paper aging into gold and two puncture wounds at the left margin as if Loy had entertained, and then abandoned, a crude binding. *Electric Prayer* for our shattered era, *etc. Etc* underlined emphatically twice.

Power. Force animating. In this philosophical mode Loy contrasts *conceptions of events* with *events per se,* providing the example of a woman starving to death. She proposes that as we read about the woman her suffering holds our entire attention, leads us to contemplate the social injustice of such a tragedy. In contrast, in the *event per se* of starving to death there is no energy to comprehend anything beyond *my shoulder blades are bobbing through my jersey dress* and the awareness that it would be as *impossible to extract a peso out of anybody as to travel to the moon.* Starving to death, a person *feels nothing but an awful fool*—

Convention asks each of us to behave as if we have constant volume, but this is a misunderstanding of the movableness of the I, its lacy, fictive nature—

Against skylike washes of ethereal gray-blues float gray-blue beings. Incipient human forms emerging from snail shells. Disembodied cherub heads with wings. Hands juggling stars. For this series of paintings Loy completes in 1932 and shows at Levy's gallery in 1933, she creates a new medium made of sand, plaster, gesso—a mixture of animal glue binder, usually rabbit skin—chalk, and white pigment.

A light leap over nothing, into nothing. The faces Loy paints in blue mirror the profiles she sketches in the margins of her manuscripts.

1925

As soon as I pick one "I" up, try it on, I discard it to pick up another, try that one on, and discard it too. I do this in front of a mirror while tying the yellow dress's halter behind my neck. Too gauzy for winter, throw a faux fur coat over. I do this walking down the street, pausing near the park. I do this faster and faster, and yet there remains the sensation of a consistent "I" doing the picking up, the trying on, the discarding. How much weight, veracity, importance to give this sensation is impossible to determine.

The bones at the crown swirl open to create an oculus as turquoise water flows through. At other times beads of water slowly drip. What happens when you look to the space between each bead? Bergson pronounced in his 1896 *Matière et mémoire,* "We become conscious of an act *sui generis* by which we detach ourselves from the present in order to replace ourselves, first, in the past in general, then, in a certain region of the past—a work of adjustment, something like the focusing of a camera." There, the mind camera-like focuses, sees into the general past and finds specific instances of "what it was like." Bergson tightening his ribbon necktie.

I focus my camera-mind on bedroom wallpaper printed with Kate Greenaway's Victorian girls in floral empire dresses. And then on a 1950s Hoover Christmas ad featuring a wasp-waist housewife in a green-and-white dressing gown sprawled childlike on the floor before her new red vacuum. And then on a nostalgic recreation of this ad in yesterday's social media feed. As mysterious as an electron jumping orbit. Shift to a Greenaway girl's bonnet ribbons tied under the chin, a big blue bow. Shift to shapeware made to be worn under a green and white robe. In 1925 "recycle," "capital flow," and "consumer credit" enter the lexicon.

I don my faux Turkish fox over an unseasonably thin dress to create a Mina Loy—or Myrna Loy—type woman. Psychically I'm all Hannah Höch collage, machine arms stuck to a Siren's body. While the interior remains private, for the outfit to work does it matter whether I style myself as Mina Loy, born December 27, 1882, with the name Mina Gertrude Lowy in a North London suburb or as Myrna Loy, born August 2, 1905, as Myrna Adele Williams in Helena, Montana? In her early twenties Williams changed her last name to Loy at the suggestion of a wild Russian writer who'd found his way to Hollywood. This man, let us call him Sasha, let us give him a shock of white hair and sand-colored eyes, could have been Mina Loy's lover when, after a summer in Vienna, 1922—sketching Freud's portrait as he read some of her prose—she moves to Berlin and stays there until relocating to Paris in spring of 1923.

Burke's description of this Berlin period has Loy enrolling Joella in the Potsdam dance school run by Isadora Duncan's sister. She installs Giulia the nurse and little Fabi nearby, and Giles is in the Caribbean with Haweis. Members of the New York crowd—Robert McAlmon, Barnes, Abbott, and Hartley—had by 1922 flocked to the half-famished, half-neon city along with political exiles like Emma Goldman and Alexander Berkman. Russian émigré artists Wassily Kandinsky, Maxim Gorky, Alexander Archipenko, Vladimir Mayakovsky, and Marina Tsvetaeva are joined by Duncan and her husband, the Russian poet Sergei Yesenin. During this period Loy takes an unnamed Russian lover, studies drawing under Archipenko, and begins the essay on Stein's prose that will be published in 1924 over the course of two issues of the *Transatlantic Review,* edited by Ford Madox Ford. Loy theorizes Stein's writing as a *literary conclusion* of Bergson's *flux of Being* before proposing a democratic modernist aesthetic, for *The flux of life is pouring its aesthetic aspect into your eyes, your ears—and you ignore it because you are looking for your canons of beauty in some sort of frame or glass case or tradition.*

In 1925 the standard conceptions of space and time are dismissed, leaning backward into the silver traumas of ancestors and forward into a location wherein the present is metaphorical. A set of figures and conventions. A gold sylph with a lobster tail spreading enamel-and-diamond wings to fill a dog collar plaque. Space had, after all, only recently begun to bend.

– o — O — o –

In 1925 the Caucasian bison, wanderer of the Carpathian Mountains, goes extinct. The first Surrealist exhibition opens in Paris at the Galerie Pierre Colle and features Hans Arp, Paul Klee, Man Ray, Max Ernst, Pablo Picasso, Joan Miró, Giorgio de Chirico, André Masson, and Pierre Roy. Benito Mussolini asserts his right to supreme power in Italy. Unchallenged, he fuses the state and the Fascist party, operating openly as the dictator Il Duce. In 1925 *The Great Gatsby* is published and is considered a commercial failure. Mount Rushmore is dedicated in South Dakota. In 1925 the Ku Klux Klan holds a parade in Washington, DC, with an estimated thirty to thirty-five thousand marchers. Adolf Hitler publishes Volume 1 of *Mein Kampf.* Malcolm X, Frantz Fanon, and Margaret Thatcher are born. A bus accident leaves eighteen-year-old Frida Kahlo with a broken spinal column, a broken collarbone, broken ribs, a broken pelvis, eleven fractures in her right leg, a crushed and dislocated right foot, and a dislocated shoulder. An iron handrail pierces her abdomen and her uterus. In 1925 John Logie Baird invents a mechanical device that projects the shadow of a doll on the other side of a room; a year later he will unveil the precursor to the modern television. The Sears, Roebuck and Company mail order catalogue sells the Thompson submachine gun for $175. The 1925 *Exposition internationale des arts décoratifs et industriels modernes* presents architecture, interior decoration, furniture, glass, jewelry created in the *Style Moderne,* which will first be called *Art Deco* in the 1960s. In Dayton, Tennessee, biology teacher John T. Scopes is arrested, indicted, and found guilty for teaching Charles Darwin's theory of evolution. Louis Armstrong forms the Hot Five and makes his first records. The Bauhaus school moves to Dessau. In 1925 the ship carrying Josephine Baker and the cast of *La revue nègre* is alerted to a German mine in the area. Baker remembers the passengers "put on life jackets, boats are unhooked, sailors work quietly . . . there would probably be a boat for our deck if there were enough to go around, but we would be last to leave ship. . . . Gathering by the railing, we began to sing. The same songs our ancestors had sung on the slave ships that carried them to America." Alone on the barren North Sea island of Heligoland, Werner Heisenberg develops the mathematical tables that will substantiate the theory of quantum mechanics, replacing the idea that atoms consist of tiny electrons like planets orbiting the sun with the idea of electrons moving in diffuse, cloud-like waves.

– o — O — o –

Tiny flower petals and leaves cut from advertisements, wrapping paper, and pochoir pattern books cover the writing desk—waiting to be glued into bouquets against gold paper scattered with gold stars. Then varnished, then set in gilded Louis Philippe frames found at the Marché aux Puces. As with the designs of René Lalique, these images spike at the edges because nature simultaneous with birth arrows toward death. The Cubist collage merges with Victorian pressed flowers until wasps and predatory beetles are as worthy of beauty as the gentle butterfly. And the strident peacock entwines with the snake's sinuous line.

Titled *Jaded Blossoms* and brought to New York City to be exhibited and sold in department story galleries—Macy's and A. I. Namm & Son—by Laurence Vail, Loy's friend from Florence newly married to Peggy Guggenheim, the collages pay for a Paris apartment large enough to include Joella, Fabi, and Giulia. The success leads to Guggenheim's investment in the lamp shop Loy will open the following year at 52 rue du Colisée.

Japanese lanterns and silk cherry blossom garlands sway from the ceiling of the shop, now a sushi restaurant. The collages' cheap materials and fragile nature mean no surviving *Jaded Blossoms* are known. No photographs either are known, but might the Beinecke's collection of Carl Van Vechten's nine-thousand-plus prints contain a Macy's window display floating several *Jaded Blossoms* behind glass? See the flowers whorl under gold stars, overlayered by a ghostly reflection of the photographer, the blur of a passing car.

When Mina opens the apartment's French doors, the smallest wind scatters petals and leaves and the sound of the VIe arrondissement waking to day floats in. Joella is asleep in her room in the back, her smocked nightgown a bit too *fillette* for seventeen. Perhaps she wears it as camouflage, and I don't blame her, often think, "Never let them know you're capable, or they'll squeeze from you every minute of your waking life. Any desire you have to create something of your own will be negated." After having been shown only once how to zigzag the leaves, Joella's cutwork is perfect. Mina gives her the best pair of shears, retreats to the balcony to smoke.

On the other side of the room behind a wall constructed of flea market birdcages, five-year-old Fabi, wrapped in Mina's kimono, sleeps. Embroidered dragonflies and rust-colored mums. Nuzzled by Bijoux, her Russian blue cat. She meets her father at the bottom of the sea where they drink tea from seashell cups. He presents her with a necklace of coral and pearls, his face a soft blur. I can imagine him pushing a small body aloft on a swing, although I, like his compatriots, never see the word "father" within his face. This I know is also said of the word "mother" and Mina and me. Categories have little traction for I am a wing's transparency, its vein tracery replicated in thinly sliced opal and gold.

Light slings low across the library's sunken garden accentuating the divots Noguchi cut into the tilting sun disk and the risk his cube takes balancing on its corner. The 1926 exhibition of Brâncuși's sculptures that Duchamp arranges in New York City profoundly influences twenty-two-year-old Noguchi. Unlocked by *Bird in Flight—an incandescent curve / licked by chromatic flames*—as Loy describes the sculpture in 1922. Unfastened by *The Newborn,* a gleaming marble egg sliced on the side, first felt in the mouth, tongue, on the palate, and then in the gut. Heavy and smooth and rounded like no hunger and no fullness a human had ever known.

Within the year Noguchi is awarded a Guggenheim Fellowship to study sculpture in Paris. At Le Dôme he meets McAlmon, who introduces him to Brâncuși, and for five months Noguchi serves as his studio assistant. Working in silence or to African music records on the phonograph Brâncuși had made with two arms playing simultaneously on different grooves. Brâncuși all in white, beard white, two white dogs whom he feeds milk.

I open the only file folder marked with the title of Loy's verse epic "Anglo-Mongrels and the Rose"—just two sheets of browning notebook paper. Handwritten on front and back. Undated, titled "Different phrases in composing a poem" and signed *M. Loy*. The paper's blue lines have faded to the palest of turquoise, ragged at the edge where the pages were torn out, two rusted punctures where there once had been a staple. Here Loy reworks the same stanza twelve times—*an effulgent iris—an elongate iris—a lucid iris*. The complete poem, Loy's most ambitious, won't appear as a continuous work until sixteen years after her death, reconstructed via the publications in which it was serialized.

The 1923 "Exiles Number" of Margaret Anderson and Jane Heap's *The Little Review,* edited by Pound, publishes the first nine pages of the poem. Cover by Fernand Léger, a wood-block bird, elongated neck. This portion tells the story of a character based on Loy's father, a Jewish Hungarian named Exodus, his apprenticeship as a tailor and his emigration from Budapest to London. It is preceded by Stein's poems and is interrupted, halfway through, by reproductions of Léger's geometric planes. Fractured cheeks, buttocks, breasts. The "Exiles Number" also includes writing by Ernest Hemingway, E. E. Cummings, H. D., McAlmon, and Dorothy Shakespear.

The next installment of Loy's epic follows in *The Little Review*'s autumn–winter 1923–1924 bilingual "French Number" edited by Heap. A character based on Loy's mother named Ada or "the English Rose" weds Exodus and gives birth to Loy's alter ego, Ova. Two plates of artwork by Robert Delaunay interrupt the poem, and the issue includes writing by Tzara, Paul Éluard, Louis Aragon, Philippe Soupault, Pierre Reverdy—untranslated—along with reproductions of work by Max Ernst, Man Ray, Hans Arp, Juan Gris, and André Masson. Surrealists at the forefront of Surrealism—Breton's first manifesto will not be published until later that year. Aside from Heap's editorial commentary, Loy's is the only work in the issue by a woman and is given more pages than any other writer.

Also in 1923 the first three stanzas of the poem appear under the title "English Rose" in *Lunar Baedecker* [*sic*], the first of two books Loy publishes in her lifetime. Part of McAlmon's Paris-based Contact Publishing Company's first series, *Lunar Baedecker* keeps company with Bryher's *Two Selves*, William Carlos Williams's *Spring and All*, Marsden Hartley's *Twenty-Five Poems*, Hemingway's *2 Stories & 10 Poems*, and McAlmon's *Post-Adolescence*. The press announces its allegiance "to the idea that artists need not please either money-making publishers, or a main street public."

The final section of Loy's epic appears in the 1925 *Contact Collection of Contemporary Writers,* a 364-page anthology which includes work by Barnes, Bryher, H. D., Ford, Havelock Ellis, James Joyce, Pound, Stein, and Williams, among others. Loy's sequence details coming into consciousness, into language and aesthetic sensibility, and into Victorian enculturation of class, gender, and racial strictures. Loy introduces baby Esau Penfold, based on Haweis, and baby Colossus, based on Cravan, as contrasts to Ova's stifled upbringing.

In 1982 Jonathan Williams's Jargon Society publishes *The Last Lunar Baedeker,* edited by Roger Conover. Peacock-blue wrapper, wine-red lettering. Here, the poem is complete, spans sixty-four pages. The most comprehensive collection of Loy's poetry to date, the volume is nearly impossible to find by the autumn I begin graduate school and the World Trade Center falls. I've known nobody in my new city for longer than a week, and a teacher photocopies for me "Anglo-Mongrels and the Rose"—then out of print, still out of print—from her copy of *Baedeker*.

—along lone ago lag lo—goner loner morsel solemn lemon ogres long ego gem ore—

eros ore eros ore eros ore—

Corner staple now rusted, the photocopy travels to Los Angeles to Mexico City to Pennsylvania to New York to Paris to Bucharest to Budapest to New Haven, boxed and unboxed with my books. Slipped into my backpack or carry-on. In Budapest I read the poem in cafés, in museums, in gardens, in the solariums of the city's Art Nouveau thermal baths. In nearly every memory I'm alone. Alone in an abandoned Moorish revival synagogue in Budapest where I sit on the only chair to read of Budapest where Loy's wealthy and refined great-grandfather had *erected a synagogue / for the people* and disinherits his son when he marries a woman from a lower class. This son dies young, leaving his own son, Exodus, in the hands of his mother, who remarries within the working class. Exodus *flowered precociously* but was apprenticed to abusive foster parents as he learned the skills of a tailor. At eighteen he immigrates to London. His daughter Ova will be *thrust / into her baby-pelisse / of ruby plush.*

The Lalique-like spikey *i*'s. The Brâncuși-smooth *oos* and *ush*—

Unguarded and derelict since the Second World War, the synagogue where I sat reading Loy's epic was a jeweled box with red and blue walls painted with gold arabesques rendered no less luminous by the pigeons entering via broken windows and the floor bereft of its mosaic. A deportation point in 1941 for twenty thousand Jews—all eventually sent to Kamianets-Podilskyi in Ukraine. In 2021 EU funds immaculately restore the synagogue.

The Budapest synagogue moves into the reading room now far too warm. I place the poem draft into its manila folder, slide it into its document box, and return it to the service counter. "The reading room," Mina says as we ascend the stairs, "I find elegant but a bit drab, although the tower of books," she says, "I very much like. A simultaneous counterbalance and acceptance of the fact that nature putrefies beginning at the edges, then seeps entirely through. Only then is the creative spirit revealed. I fill my sitting room with potted palms, ivy trained up the mantle, garden furniture instead of horse-hair sofas. Division between interior and exterior dissolved."

I exit in Paris, walking through the Puces looking for the spikey opal stars and bat wings of the Lalique anklet Natalie Barney had received from Liane de Pougy. Diamonds catching the light. Little bats done in blue enamel swooping past poppies caught in amber just before dying, their leaves sun-scorched. In 1925 Lalique cascaded through opera houses, museums, salons, restaurants, cafés; pinned to coats, nestled in hair, fastened around necks, ankles, wrists. Natalie bending to touch the sharp points of wings, silk stockings snagged.

– o — O — o –

Paris erects a city at the center of the city—a white cubist dream city spanning Right and Left Bank, 1925. Motifs pressed into white plaster and picked out in gold. Or unmarked planes like Le Corbusier's *Pavillon de l'esprit nouveau.* Along the Pont Alexandre III spanning the Seine: a row of bijou shops. One window frames a single mannequin arm gloved in soft pink leather, touch of fur. The next, a tortoiseshell cigarette case and lighter inlaid with silver lightning bolts. Then Sonia Delaunay's simultaneous scarf. At night the white dream bursts into light. Eiffel Tower aswirl with Citroën's red and gold, and at the center of the exposition: *Les sources de France,* Lalique's four-story fountain erected of glass panes held aloft by 128 glass caryatids who flow and drape, bodies and faces gentle.

The door to the perfumier opens to Shalimar's exquisite bergamot, vanilla, iris, and leather. The saleswoman outfitted in La Garçonne's tailored navy-blue coat raises the crystal bottle to anoint the wrist, the soft divot behind the ears, the nape of the neck. Even as taffetas appear in plaids, checks, and stripes, everyone is talking about the future of gray. When we used white powder and pink rouge, gray was all very well, but modern powder is ochre, yellow, cream, mauve. Rouge is raspberry, mulberry, orange. As they paint watch dials, the radium girls lick the tips of their brushes to give them fine points. The adventurous among them doing up their nails, cheekbones, and eyelids with the green glow.

Hold a Shalimar-wrist to the nose. Lounge in a fur coat and t-strap shoes on a funhouse floor painted with a Coney Island beach scene. An enormous wall-size gilt frame holds a mirror, angled to create the impression of being inside a framed photograph of bathers at the sea.

In *La revue nègre,* Josephine Baker makes her entrance wearing little more than a string of pearls and a skirt made of 16 rubber bananas. Taking center stage, her movement is part Charleston, part belly dance. Beauty editors suggest rubbing walnut oil on skin to darken it until Bakerskin and the hair pomade Baker Fix arrive on the market. The next act to open at the Théâtre des Champs-Élysées is Anna Pavlova, presenting her infamous four-minute ballet, *Dying Swan*. Immortalized on film in 1925, she performs the dance over four thousand times.

1919

From Salina Cruz to Valparaíso then on to Santiago and the 875-mile journey by train to Buenos Aires. This journey and the five months—November to late March—that Loy spends in Buenos Aires fill just five pages of her biography. Passages from artist and collector Katherine Dreier's memoir of her own stay in Argentina during this period supplement the little known about Loy, pregnant, broke, hoping for news of Cravan—and recognition from his wealthy mother that she is his wife. During this time Loy composes the first version of her political tract *Psycho-Democracy: A movement to focus human reason on THE CONSCIOUS DIRECTION OF EVOLUTION*. Marcel Duchamp is also in Buenos Aires, and although they are lifelong friends, there's no indication that they connect. In a letter to Moose a year later, Loy describes her voyage from Salina Cruz to Valparaíso. She doesn't mention her state of body or mind, instead recounts *the dainty fairyland* that Japanese passengers on their way to pick rice in Peru made of their third-class accommodations. The European clothes they wore upon disembarking, Loy writes, stripped them of their dignity.

– o — O — o –

Under Saturn heavy in the sky I in a fir-green caftan walk with Colossus through a forest, sun casting the illusion of fire in the trees. Our fascination feeds on simultaneously sensing ourselves to be in danger and sensing danger to be an illusion, a suburban leaf blower droning in the background.

We are on stage and walking through a cellophane forest accompanied by the dog I had tried in Mexico to find again and feed. I understand the cardinal cord-work trimming of my dress to be in homage to extinct birds. A voiceover in French says our dog is leading us to the coast where the sea exhales an iodine cure.

And then a blast. A sun-that-is-not-a-sun I push away with my right hand, palm out, fingers up like a golden icon offering benediction.

The sea now occupies a solid state. All salt and air motionless around the geese.

How thick, their flying-through, heavy with the fact that we, their guardians, had meant them for the harvester.

$$- o — O — o -$$

Mina wakes saying the sentence, "When the sky changes color somebody is dying." Buenos Aires, 1919, pregnancy dress of coral kasha, sprigs of cherry blossoms worked with white silk, and long afternoons seated on the veranda of the British consulate. Too much salt in her head, too much post-blast cinder for much thinking. The body is an ecology of processes and practices that are necessary for personhood but cannot accurately be described as a person.

Over tea, bud-painted cups and little silver spoons stamped with stars, a Mrs. So-and-So mentions Marcel living near the Teatro

Colón. She says "cigar" and "spotted on the Plaza Lavalle learning from the Mapuche women how to carve wood for his chess set." Mina writes him a note on blue-and-red checked stationery about Empress Joséphine's passion for violets—favored second only to the musk that continued to scent her dressing room decades after her death. She writes, "Did you know that Joséphine went by 'Yvette' or 'Rose' prior to Napoleon, who preferred her by her middle name? Just imagine her there in her boudoir, Marcel, silk pooling over black-and-white chessboard flooring. She makes up her face, watched intently in the mirror by the orangutan she and Napoleon dressed in infant-sized white dresses, taught to eat with a knife and fork, trained to sleep in their marital bed, and named Rose. Rose adored turnips and died within the year." Mina ends her letter: "I imagine Joséphine's grief smelled of burnt sugar cubes dropped in lemon and liquid velvet," by which he'll know she means, "Marcel, I'm here in Buenos Aires—"

In Buenos Aires Duchamp's only interest is in chess, which requires sleeping during the day, playing against himself at night. His dear brother Raymond Duchamp-Villon and *cher ami* Guillaume Apollinaire among the twenty million now dead. Chess affords a mode of making when Apollinaire becomes a cardboard cutout with an actual linen bandage splotched with real blood wrapped around his head. Birth name and father unknown, and therefore improvising, he became the bastard son of princes, prelates, and popes.

What might be "I" explodes the moment thought slips into language, swills on the palate like fine drink, then lingers on the lips even after one swallows or spits it out. Or perhaps "I" is only constructed in the act of speaking, is never anything more than a paper version. Limbs joined with brads and finished with a tulle-scrap dress. "I" walks away, down the street, even as what is more properly the self traverses the city in multiple, alternative dimensions at a variety of scales, speeds, and slownesses.

– o — O — o –

Marcel and Mina devote many Argentine afternoons to the Confitería Las Violetas. There they discuss the inclination of art to corrupt into the commercial. The café's floors are Italian tile, and the spindle-legged chairs are well spaced between the columns trimmed with gilding. Sun sparks through sparkling stained glass to land on cakes and demitasse cups. "An homage to Paris," Mina says through the cigar smoke, "and an educated eye cannot simply view the candied pear in and of itself"—pointing to the lovely *Poires belle Hélène* before her. "No, the eye views the rotting pear as candied, the candied pear as rotted and quick-calculates the price-point of each with the understanding that in Market A the aesthetic of candied is in, rotted is out. While in Market B the aesthetic of rotted is in, and candied is out. As such, the eye and its attached mind are chained to education's neon tassels and signs."

On walks through the park, Mina leans heavy on Marcel's arm as he pretends away her pregnancy. Neither the rotted nor the candied, the faience nor the wad of trash, the just-born or the newly dead, the male nor the female nor the nonbinary is superior. All modalities are equally susceptible to brand and marketability. All modalities pass away. At night, more often than not, Mina wins at chess.

I want this, want Mina and Marcel to discover each other in Buenos Aires, want them to walk together there or at least years later, nearly a decade later, to linger late at Le Dôme as Marcel admits to having known Mina was in Buenos Aires penniless, pregnant, Colossus having vanished, and she living only by the grace of the consulate. Confess with his sly-sphinx smile, offering no reason for not having extended himself to her.

Mina doesn't confess that she had watched him exit a shop alone and quite melancholy as she thought, "Ah, yes. There he is. My

Marcel." Then quickly crossed to the opposite side of the street, relieved at the camouflage of pregnancy.

While being Mrs. Arthur Cravan has cachet in certain artistic circles, being Mrs. Fabian Avenarius Lloyd may have secured in Buenos Aires what was necessary for a woman who needed to live by her own cleverness. With its Lloyds of London affiliation, Fabian's name was surely worth satin for two dresses on credit, one pair of shoes on credit, a fringed shawl, a pot of Jonteel face cream, a pair of lace gloves, a long strand of imitation pearls—relished for luxury only after making use of their ability to construct the type of woman someone feeds a proper meal.

Mina draws a looping motion with her hand, describing the fall of the pearls as Marcel nods along, recalling Buenos Aires draped in a gray mist.

"As for me," Mina says quoting Marcel back to Marcel while lighting one of his Habana cigars, "an artist must be alone with himself, as in a shipwreck."

Duchamp is known to have made three works in Buenos Aires. *Unhappy Readymade*—a wedding gift for his sister, the artist Suzanne Duchamp—is a geometry book accompanied by a letter instructing that it should be hung outside so the wind could "choose its own problems." Two stereoscope photographs of the sea on which he drew a pyramid floating on the water. And a study for a section of *The Large Glass* titled *To Be Looked at (from the Other Side of the Glass) with One Eye, Close to, for Almost an Hour.* This 20 ⅛ × 16 ¼ inch shattered glass panel is etched with a large pyramid composed of thin red, green, and yellow horizontal lines accompanied by a pointed vertical column made of brass topped by a small, round magnifying glass haloed with concentric circles.

Entering Gallery 508 on MoMA's fifth floor, I approach *To Be Looked at* as if I am alone in the room. I place my eye as close as I can to the magnifying glass.

– o — O — o –

Le printemps. The March air of 1919 singes rose-gold as Mina travels back to Surrey by sea. Back to mother Julia, corset busks creaking, chintz curtains scattered with prevaricating rosebuds, living at the height of bourgeois dream in a house she calls Burnside.

On the boat sea sickness and morning sickness build and then cancel each other out, sailing away from the Americas as Emiliano Zapata rides through the gates of a hacienda near his family home. The guards lift their rifles to the sky, send off shots in a grand salute. As he dismounts his horse, a bugle sounds three times in a show of respect. Silence. Even the cicadas and sparrows stop. And prior to the birds and bugs taking up again their song, the guards lift their rifles and gun Zapata down.

Of Valparaíso Mina knows only alias, vapor, parasol, avail—ova, pair, lava, vail—voila, viola, rival, lair—sap, ore, savior—

Of Buenos Aires Mina knows only ebonies, sunrise, bruise—anise, eosin, neurosis—bun, bear, unbear—see, sea, brine, bare, bones—

Of Surrey she knows only rue, ruse—user, sue—err, err, err.

Delivered back to the brick boxes of middle-class British domesticity, sister over endless games of bridge saying, "Glass is so dear these days, make sure to dry it with a special Irish linen cloth," and,

"Beneath skin dulled by anxiety or neglect is the soft, exquisite complexion of youth waiting to be restored by Ven-Yusa oxygen face cream," and, "Should husbands love secrets? I have bought a whole host of beautiful silk Union Jacks mounted on little gilt-topped rods and standing ten inches high. *Just* the thing to decorate our victory dinner, tea, and supper tables."

Mina devotes her mind-entire to the kaleidoscopic back of the Bijou playing cards.

Afternoons, she drags the garden chair under the cherry tree to stare at the bare branches willing them to bud. The garden walls she wills to dissolve into the green Swiss hills of Rudolf von Laban's Tanzfarm at Monte Verità near Ascona. There, Laban stands in orange robe and sandals slightly down-meadow from five female dancers. Two are striking, nude—one very dark-skinned, one very light. Their bodies in all other ways exquisitely match as they rise slowly to the balls of their feet, muscular and gleaming as if oiled for the sun.

Eyes closed, arms lifted to the weak British winter sun, Mina sees herself there in the field, her arms as if encircling a basket. Bending at her waist she becomes a crescent moon. Bare feet anchored to earth, hands reaching to the horizon, hips in the opposite direction, pulling away from herself until giving in to rush like a river across the field. Two women in gold tunics ignited by gong sounds shiver and shake, their energy generated from within just as with a flower, a beetle, a stone. Every line, form, color has risen from a land of silence.

Black walls, blue ceiling—chairs for fifty are squeezed around a performance platform at Zurich's Cabaret Voltaire. The two gold tunic women from the Tanzfarm take the stage wearing enormous papier-mâché masks—the blue Catching Flies Mask on the right, the yellow Nightmare Mask on the left. To a gong they perform a flickering dance called *The Butterflies of Ensor*. Their finish involves ecstatic whirling and makes way for Sophie Taeuber. She vibrates and shudders in a hundred-jointed dance, a movement of fragments and angles calling forth Monte Verità's sun, flashes and edges full of dazzle as Hugo Ball recites "Song to the Flying Fish and the Sea Horses," raw syllables mounting and trilling.

Body become animal, mineral, plant, ocean, atmosphere, galaxy.

The movableness of the I, its lacy, fictive nature.

April sun streams red through Burnside's terrible brocade as Jemima Fabienne Cravan Lloyd slips, a little moon from her mother's womb. Fabi, Fabienne, the daughter of Fabian Avenarius Lloyd, father in absentia. A trio of photobooth photos taken twenty years later shows Fabi wearing close-cropped bangs, just as she did as a little girl in a photograph Berenice Abbott took. By 1939 she has her father's face, holds it in a smile. Then, in the next shot she holds it in a blur—flesh become photograph paper, silver, and air.

– o — O — o –

By 1919's deep spring, Loy's traded Surrey for Geneva. She does this for Fabi, calling on Dr. and Mrs. Henri Grandjean, Cravan's esteemed stepfather and mother living in the best neighborhood while on the other side of the city the League of Nations is being born. The swinging curves of Jugendstil are present, but, of uneven width, they mass in nervous tension. The house façade swells outward, restless, wanting to embrace Fabi for its own regardless of whether its owners will decide to be home when Mina calls.

When she's not practicing her how-do-you-do and doesn't-she-look-just-like-Fabian, Mina walks along the promenade with Emily

Greene Balch, talking suffrage and government. Talking about *Democracy of The Spirit,* which she's been detailing in *Psycho-Democracy's* proposal for government via creative imagination.

Over the next two years Loy expands and publishes this tract in more versions than any other piece of her writing. She will send a two-page signed typescript to Moose in 1920. She will fold and mail a small broadside to Carl Van Vechten. A short pamphlet she will have printed in Florence and sign *Mina Loy / Mexico. Buenos Aires. Surrey. Geneva. / Florence 1917–1919.* She will publish a six-page manifesto in *The Little Review*'s Brâncuși number in Autumn, 1921, signed *Mina Loy, Buenos Aires, 1918.*

The Little Review's version is bisected by four of Brâncuși's full-page photographs of his brass *Mlle Pogany* sculpture. The photos are inserted after Loy's description of *Life* as *luminous bodies, knocking sparks off one another in chaos* and before her description of class as a psychological condition imposed by the elite dominant minority to deprive the impoverished majority of power. The series of photos renders Mlle Pogany rather alien—large forehead, metal ridges down her spine, skin blossoming star-like with light.

The café mirror shows Mina's head to have been replaced by Mlle Pogany's blossom of light. The room's abuzz with the Palace of Versailles and the treaty drawn up by the US, Great Britain, France, and Italy requiring Germany to take full responsibility for starting the war by paying reparations, surrendering ten percent of its territory, and handing over all overseas colonies. The Austro-Hungarian empire of Loy's Jewish-Hungarian father has been dissolved, and the last emperor exiles in Switzerland. Mina scans the Café of Birds for his bear-skin coat, lining stitched with diamonds. As she drops one-two-three cubes of sugar in her tea, Béla Kun's Hungarian-Soviet Republic collapses, the Romanian army occupies Budapest, and the Danube is colored violet with blood.

Tsk-tsk say the Swiss drinking caffè crema in their precise yet hearty way: nothing good can come of this, and Mina is nodding along, quoting from her tract—militarism *Sustains the belligerent masculine social ideal. Like all concentrated human forces it is psychically magnetic*—although her mother's magazines continue babbling in her blood. They suggest that perhaps she's overlooked a thing that men just cannot accept. Perhaps she's failed to ensure the perfect daintiness that's impossible when there's the least trace of the odor or moisture of perspiration. Her own underarm glands, she must understand, perpetually threaten to activate, and the curve of her arm, which her gentlemen friends find so inviting, prevents rapid evaporation. The result: others become aware of her nervousness in the form of a subtle stink that she might not herself perceive but that nevertheless reveals what disgusts all proper gentlemen—her animality.

Mina drowns this voice out by focusing very hard on Emily, her little bow-mouth, intelligent eyes, round glasses. Emily says something about full women's suffrage approved in the Netherlands! And for certain classes in Belgium! And the US Congress approving the 19th Amendment that grants women the right to vote! Emily is saying this and punctuating facts by rapping the floor with her walking stick. Someone who looks like Charles I's beloved Empress Zita, the last Empress of Austria and Queen of Hungary, joins the conversation.

Europe, Mina decides then and there, is a hereditary disease that along with its big red child, North America, makes a test subject of its closest kin. This Sophie Taeuber and the other Dadaists understand, renting the Kaufleuten Hall for what will be their final Zurich event. Music by Arnold Schoenberg and Erik Satie. Laban ladies float through the audience in their African masks. Someone reads an offensive essay called "Final Dissolution" to a headless tailor's dummy as the audience tears the auditorium apart.

– o — O — o –

In 1919 the Treaty of Versailles is signed, ending World War I. In the US, Emma Goldman is jailed for distributing pamphlets about contraception and is deported to the Soviet Union. The Volstead Act is passed, establishing prohibition in the US. During the summer of 1919 hundreds of African-Americans are killed and thousands injured in race riots and lynchings. In Germany, Adolf Hitler gives his first speech for the German Workers' Party as severe inflation sees the Papiermark rise against the US dollar. Benito Mussolini establishes the Italian National Fascist Party. The Egyptian Revolution begins. Babe Ruth is traded by the Boston Red Sox to the New York Yankees for $25,000—the largest sum ever paid for a player at this time. In 1919 the average annual American income in the US is $1,518. Charlie Chaplin, Mary Pickford, Douglas Fairbanks, and D. W. Griffith launch United Artists Corporation, intended to allow artists independence from commercial studios. The pop-up toaster, the shortwave radio, and the arc welder are invented. The last sighting is recorded of Appalachian Barbara's buttons—a member of the sunflower family. Duchamp pencils a moustache and beard on a cheap postcard of the Mona Lisa, titles it *L.H.O.O.Q.* In Weimar, Germany, Walter Gropius founds the Bauhaus, which he envisions as a utopian craft guild uniting painting, architecture, and sculpture. André Breton and Philippe Soupault write *Les champs magnétiques,* the first book of automatic writing. Eileen Gray designs her "Dragons" armchair, and Sylvia Beach opens her Shakespeare and Company bookshop in Paris.

– o — O — o –

Under the sway of Saturn, clarity is born of the head vaporized or vanished or turned into a cloud. A failed star of the slowest revolution. A planet of detour, delay, melancholia, as Saturn is depicted by Albrecht Dürer in *Melencolia I*, 1514, engraved on copper, printed on laid paper, and displayed in a heavy gilt frame. The emaciated dog Mina loved in Mexico sleeps at Melancholy's feet between the granite sphere she once carved and a polyhedron she has abandoned.

Her head a cloud, a vapor, soft liquid fire, Mina floods with the electrostatic energy of Sophie Taeuber's hundred-jointed dance until she reaches Florence at the end of summer. On her way from the station she stops in the shade to watch two gorgeous children run up the street toward her. The girl: all dark gold and blue coat. The boy: all black hair and abandon. And watching them she almost forgets the haunting questions: "Why is Melancholy's dog half-starved?" and "Why did I let Arthur Cravan drown?" But it is not until they cry "Mamma" and then "Mina" does she recognize Joella, twelve, and Giles, ten, running up Costa San Giorgio to lead her home. So picturesque they are, but instead of following she makes her way to the river. Fabi swaddled to her chest, she spends the night on the Ponte Vecchio, the only bridge over the Arno that the Germans will not destroy as the midsection of Italy burns and fascism rises across Europe.

I dream Saturn's eight rings, each orbiting at a different speed as I Cassini-float in the 2,920-mile gap between Ring A and Ring B. The rings are composed of pieces of comets, asteroids, and shattered moons that tore apart before reaching the planet.

– o — O — o –

Sliding Loy's 1919 *Auto-Facial-Construction* advertising pamphlet out of its gray-blue protective folder, I'm stunned by the hot-pink silk covering the boards of the case its previous owner had once comissioned to keep its contents safe. Book plate: Yale University Library, gift of Mable Dodge Luhan, Lux et Veritas, 1952. Breath held over the pamphlet—five small pages hand-bound with a white silk thread, title inked a deep pink, printed in Florence by Tipografia Giuntina. To be read without touching any more than is necessary. Inked in black: *Mina Loy. Sociétaire du Salon d'Automne, Paris. The face is our most potent symbol of personality* Loy begins, ending with an offer to instruct potential clients in an *esoteric anatomical science.* This instruction will, the pamphlet admits, be expensive. But isn't it worth the price, this method to strip away the commodity-face bestowed by time, restoring the adolescent's *facial contours* which always had been *in harmony with the conditions of his soul?*

1965

Assemblages—

Snow Crop, ca. 1955. The lids of fourteen tin cans are mounted on a muddy, white board, 25 × 19 3/16 inches. All but two are rusted. One of these is shiny; the other has "Snow Crop Orange Juice" stamped across the silhouette of a white mountain against a Bayer-Blue background. The lids aren't arranged in a rigid pattern but are nevertheless balanced compositionally. Five are set in loose, vertical lines down both the right and left sides of the work. A cluster at the top left communicates with absence at the center.

Untitled, ca. 1955. On an 18-inch, square copper background painted with flecks of blue and rose, four flat, rusted metal disks perforated with round concentric cutouts are arranged around a circular gear, placed precisely in the middle of the field. The disks are perhaps remnants of the machines that pulled silver from the Rocky Mountains.

Untitled, ca. 1955. Two warped metal disks mounted on cardboard, 24 ½ × 15 inches. Weathered, corrugated ribs. A star has torn through the top disk, ripping open the circumference as it passed. Acid seems to have burned the center of the lower disk away.

Constructed in Aspen, where Loy continues gathering rummage just as she's done since the late '40s while living on the Bowery. She fills the front room of her apartment with egg crates, rags, feathers, tin cans, bits of wire, metal, and string. Trash transported to art, these *refusées* are Loy's only known nonfigurative pieces and her latest preserved works.

In 1965 the US increases military forces in South Vietnam and begins Operation Rolling Thunder, an aerial bombardment campaign over North Vietnam which will last until 1968, killing more than fifty-two thousand people. In 1965 most of Congress and much of the US support the war, although tens of thousands attend the antiwar teach-in at the University of California at Berkeley. Half the population of the US is under twenty-five. Eva Hesse is awarded a year-long fellowship in an abandoned textile factory in Germany and begins to move into the three-dimensional space of found objects and papier-mâché. By the end of her residency, she will consider herself a sculptor. Carolee Schneemann teaches herself how to make films. Signing the 1965 Social Security Act, Lyndon B. Johnson establishes Medicare and Medicaid. David Bowie, still going by David Jones, records "I Pity the Fool/Take My Trip" with The Mannish Boys, and Twiggy has her first fashion shoot. In France, married women are given the right to work without their husbands' approval. Beginning above the Pacific Ocean near Hawaii and ending over the Gulf of Mexico, the first American spacewalk lasts twenty-three minutes. The Watts Riots, also called the Watts Uprising or the Watts Rebellion, erupt in California in response to police brutality, economic deprivation, and racism. The three peaceful marches that take place from Selma, Alabama to the capital city of Montgomery to protest the suppression of Black Americans' voting rights are met with violence. Later that year the Voting

Rights Act passes. In 1965 a loaf of bread costs 21 cents; a new house costs $13,600. The Beatles make their second concert tour of the US and release *Help!* and *Rubber Soul*. A quartet that had called themselves The Warlocks, then The Falling Spikes, settles on The Velvet Underground. In 1965 Malcolm X is assassinated. T. S. Eliot, Martin Buber, Winston Churchill, Le Corbusier, and Jack Spicer die. J. K. Rowling, Dr. Dre, and Björk are born. Named after Eliza Doolittle from George Bernard Shaw's *Pygmalion*, ELIZA, the first chatbot, is developed at MIT. When users attribute human feelings to the program, ELIZA's creator is surprised. Sylvia Plath's *Ariel* is published two years after her death. *Days of Our Lives* debuts, *Doctor Zhivago* starring Omar Sharif premiers, and *My Fair Lady* wins eight Academy Awards. Jean-Luc Godard's *Alphaville* is released, Andrei Tarkovsky directs *Andrei Rublev*, and Sergei Parajanov releases *Shadows of Forgotten Ancestors.* The Beinecke Rare Book & Manuscript Library celebrates its two-year anniversary. In 1965 hemlines rise above the thigh; waistlines of dresses loosen to sheath and A-line styles made up in bright geometric prints and shiny synthetics. Pastel eye shadow, winged eyeliner, fake lashes, light blush, and soft pink lips are essential to mod and baby doll looks. The US Supreme Court grants married couples the legal right to contraception. Single women won't obtain this right until 1972.

A busted, silver-mining town with fewer than a thousand residents, rickety Victorians, and mud-stricken streets, the Aspen that Loy moves to in 1953 is on its way to becoming a European-style ski resort developed by a veteran of the 10th Mountain Division ski patrol and Walter Paepcke, who made his fortune manufacturing cardboard containers. In 1944 Paepcke enticed Bauhaus-trained Herbert Bayer—Joella's second husband, married that year—to move to Aspen to oversee architectural development. Bayer was the originator of the Bauhaus's signature Universal Alphabet typeface—pure geometric forms drawn with a ruler and compass. After the school's closure in 1933, he designed at least three Third Reich propaganda campaigns, although there's no evidence he embraced Nazi ideology. He immigrated to the US in 1938 with an invitation from Alfred H. Barr to design MoMA's *Bauhaus: 1919–28*.

Aspen's aspirations: more than a ski town. More than a center for business. A commercial Monte Verità expressed as the Aspen Institute for Humanistic Studies, the Aspen Skiing Company, the Aspen Music Festival and School, and the annual International Design Conference. Across forty acres of ranchland Bayer constructs over a dozen buildings, several works of landscape art, and indoor-outdoor structures for summer festivals. Fritz Benedict, Taliesin-trained and, by 1949, Fabi's second husband, codesigns the reception center along with cabins, chalets, warming huts. Introducing flat roofs, expanses of glass, and cantilevered balconies, Bayer also renovates the Victorians, the Romanesque Revival opera house, and the Hotel Jerome—painted light gray with window accents in Bayer Blue.

– o — O — o –

"Pixel," "bargaining chip," "Eurocentrism," and "biohazard" enter the dictionary in 1965. The cordless telephone, Kevlar, and mace are invented. SpaghettiOs, Apple Jacks, and Easy Cheese arrive on the market.

Carolee Schneemann's first film, *Fuses,* 1964–1966, begins with a leader of scratched green and then opens to a handheld close-up of a woman and a man making love in a dark interior. Then, outside in the distance shimmering blue and silhouetted, Schneemann, nude, walks into the sea. Then light through the window, the dark red of her pelvis, his penis, a mouth, a leg, more light flooding the curtain. Her black cat watches from the window ledge, backed by leafy trees. Silhouetted, Schneemann walks into the sea, a dark interior of shoulder, her hand caressing the man's skin, the film is silent. Her head thrown back in ecstasy. Her breasts. Their bodies pumping, they make love, they kiss. Crows in a pink field, an occasional glance of unobstructed sky. Slick skin, "a woman has sex organs more or less everywhere," Luce Irigaray writes in 1985, white light, tangle of Christmas lights, tangle of limbs in blue light, blue-green field. Collaged paper, feathers, and tinting applied directly to the celluloid. The cat watches from the windowsill, the camera sees from the driver's seat of a car. The bedroom window in white light, silhouetted, Schneeman walks into the sea. The cat's fur red-black, green silk sheets, she walks into the sea.

When the film premieres at Cannes, men in the audience rip open their seats, throw the stuffing in the air.

The touch of the hand on the film's body in editing.

The jagged edge of the tin can's lid.

A sensual register—light.

Schneemann's films play on a loop in the back of a Tribeca gallery's retrospective. A couple whispers in a corner about another exhibition. Someone sits on a bench and texts.

By the time the film ends Mina's standing there alone in her black Mary Quant miniskirt dress. Claudine collar.

In a rarely seen photograph of Loy in her final years, her eyes are wild, her hair Einstein-voluminous, and she has a white moustache.

Aspen, o Aspen. To live and die in Aspen. In nape, pen, sea, spa, sap, apse, snap, span and span and span—

At the end of *Islands in the Air,* Loy's alter ego, Linda, is eighteen years old and finishing a year of art school in turn-of-the-century Munich. Unknown to her, the baroness with whom she lodges turns a profit by leaving her alone with men in potentially compromising situations. When Linda discovers this she demotes her from duenna to landlady—*You are now in a position to give me a latch-key*. Linda purchases a clay pipe ornamented with an albino fly which she carries about town—*I preferred to appear as an amateur lunatic rather than an amateur baggage.*

None of the people in this book have ever really existed—although if you look <u>into</u> them deep enough—they are all <u>the same person</u>—Loy scrawls on the back of one of her drafts.

Hannah Wilke, topless, hands out sticks of chewing gum as part of her *Starification Object Series* performance in Paris, 1975. After gallery visitors chew them, she stretches and folds the gum into labia shapes and sticks them to her face, neck, shoulders, torso.

To examine the celluloid subjected to burning, baking, cutting, painting, dipping the footage in acid, building up dense layers of collage including feathers and earth, you must infuse it with light.

– o — O — o –

The interview that Paul Blackburn and Robert Vas Dias conduct with Loy in Aspen in August 1965 streams through my headphones at the New York Public Library's Art & Architecture Reading Room as I wait for the librarian to bring out books on Hannah Wilke, Eva Hesse, Carolee Schneemann—a pantheon of Loy's unofficial goddaughters. I'm assigned a seat at a table otherwise empty except for a man reading Dafydd Jones's *The Fictions of Arthur Cravan: Poetry, Boxing, and Revolution.* While the coincidence is startling, the room's too quiet for conversation, and I'm not here for Cravan. John Ashbery to Carolyn Burke about his attempt to contact Fabi on a trip to Aspen in 1979: "The reason I wished to get in touch with her is that I'm fascinated with Arthur Cravan's poetry.... Mrs. Benedict was out when I called, and I was there too briefly to pursue it further. I have also been informed, perhaps erroneously, that she is not at all interested in her father's writings, and isn't very helpful to those that are interested in them."

Blackburn and Vas Dias had been attending the Aspen Institute's Writers Conference where Jonathan Williams—poet, Black Mountain affiliate, and founder of Jargon Press, essential to mid-century American avant-garde poetry—is, for the summer, in residence. In 1958 Williams had published *Lunar Baedeker & Time-Tables,* Loy's second book and the last she will see in her lifetime.

Her voice low and mellow, regal British accent, Loy worries her false teeth will register on the tape recorder. Should she wear them or take them out, and can you hear them clacking? Her teeth, she explains with humor, were nearly all pulled in a series of terrifying visits to the dentist when she was no more than a teenager. She then recounts her marriage to a *French celebrity* who disappeared—he'd been a poet who went *to a South American country* they were going to stay in. I take a long look at the man with the Cravan book. Late sixties. A black bandana skull-cap, black leather jacket, Le Corbusier glasses. She'd given Cravan her money *to keep in his pocket so I wouldn't lose it.* Or does she say *so I wouldn't lose him?*

When the librarian delivers Schneemann's *Imaging Her Erotics: Essays, Interviews, Projects,* I flip to her recollection of visiting Charles Olson in Gloucester, Massachusettes, in October 1963. Trained as a painter, Schneemann was beginning to explore performance and had not yet begun making films. She and her partner, composer James Tenney, had sent Olson "a collaged graceful letter with burnt edges and a compressed, admiring text" asking if they might meet him. At his house Schneemann's "early clandestine searches for the absent feminine" lead her to snoop for Olson's artist-wife Betty's dried paint brushes. She notices the long, silky strands of Betty's hair in her brush in the bathroom. Betty had left them a plate of homemade cookies but was nowhere to be found. Does Olson show them his recent edition of *Maximus Poems,* published by Jargon directly following Loy's *Baedeker?* The next day Schneemann, Tenney, and Olson walk along the shore. Tenney and Olson talk music and poetry, and when Olson asks Schneemann about her work she tells him about "wanting to take painting into real time and lived actions, even using fragments of language." He responds by reminding her that "when the cunt began to speak . . . it was the beginning of the end of Greek theater." "Was there something," Schneemann writes, "I would destroy?"

As Loy reads the most provocative passages from "Love Songs," she interrupts herself to comment gleefully on her perceived immorality and to tell about her childhood. Her angry mother. Living in Munich for art school with a baroness who *was always trying to get me into trouble.* People she knew and observed in Florence and Paris. She asks Blackburn and Vas Dias if they mind if she smokes—of course not—and she smokes. She responds to interjections made in German by the German woman who cares for her. In her eighties her mind is still sharp. Those who don't understand her references find her strange, incoherent in old age.

– o — O — o –

"The first three-dimensional magazine," *Aspen, the Magazine in a Box* contains booklets as well as phonograph recordings, posters, postcards, and reels of super-8. Stillwater Ranch, the 150-acre oasis outside of Aspen designed by Fabi's husband for them, their four children, and Fabi's pets—a Belgian Sheepdog, a Great Pyrenees, ten ducks, four finches, a peacock, two kittens, four horses, and a pony—is profiled in the inaugural issue, 1965.

Fabi is described as the famous architect's wife who helps at his office and, while she doesn't enjoy cooking, makes perfect meals for family and friends. She, however, is no common housewife. Born in Paris, the daughter of "Mina Loy, celebrated poetess of the twenties, and Arthur Cravan, proto-Dadaist and nephew of Oscar Wilde," by the time she was fourteen Fabi "had sold a painting to the Queen of England. Three years later, she was studying at the Art Students League and the Parsons School of Design in New York, developing into a free-lance designer, specializing in packaging and jewelry. Talented and precocious and still in her teens, she could count among her customers Helena Rubinstein, Lucius Beebe, Shirley Temple, Eddy Duchin, Rosalind Russell."

Stillwater Ranch refuses to impose on its natural site, follows the low, lean lines of the surrounding hills and meadows. The sod roof's sprinkler system exhales a fine mist, filling the air with rainbows. A waterfall pours into a rock-ringed pool, flowing in a stone trough around the house to the horse pasture. Bougainvillea arches through a window. In one photo a peacock poses regally on the roof.

The embankment fracture prevents us from seeing the sun.

Not far from here, Loy's grave is marked by three stacked marble disks.

– o — O — o –

Not at home at the Hotel Jerome but more or less at the European-style café, opposite. To age in America's youth-obsessed culture. In film-light. In half-light, an ongoing search for the spiritual. No longer correcting others when they misunderstand. But had Loy ever corrected others? She had long practice at not being understood, misunderstandings going unremarked partly, perhaps, because of the internalized, disciplining voice of her mother. Because she was a woman, lived in economic precarity, depended on others' generosity. But also perhaps she found pleasure and depth in the slippage—consoling Jonathan Williams who had written with worry that she was disappointed in the lack of reviews, *The best way to conquer is to wear as helmet: a smile. . . . Change from Persona Non Grata to PERSONA GOOD GRINNER.*

At that height air in the Rockies is exhilarating.

What the cells say as they age.

The first snowfall arrives in October. The last snowfall in May.

1886

Late-night TV or Netflix seeps through walls.

A barren landscape of ravens and jutting rocks. A lone woman pauses before an enormous brass cauldron suspended above a fire. She's in a long, chalk-blue dress, enchanted figures embroidered at her hem, wildflowers sashed to her waist, a snake twisting through her necklaces. Her left hand holds a crescent-shaped sickle at her hip, linking her to Hecate and the moon. With the wand in her right hand, she draws around herself and her fire a protective circle in the sand within which flowers bloom. John William Waterhouse, *Magic Circle,* 1886.

As Mina sketches she hums a little tune, placing wildflowers on the fire. Flower to feather to flesh to organ. The taffeta rustle an indication that she has, as have we all, many times in different iterations walked this earth.

Follow the canvas's green paint. It suggests blue is next to be added. Then blue demands viridian, and viridian demands kneeling within the magic circle to find there the movableness of the I, its lacy, fictive nature. A sequence of images, texts, textures, which might be as finely held as a Fabergé egg. Or as absently as the phone in one hand, the index finger of the other, scrolling.

Fruit, flowers, and foliage entwine over the dotted background of William Morris's 1886 *Lily and Pomegranate* motif. Morris & Co. produces this as wallpaper, hand-cutting each element into a separate woodblock inked with natural, mineral-based dyes, then hand-pressing these onto paper. Color by color. Element by element. Morris delivers his "Aims of Art" lecture on five occasions in 1886, warning of the tyrannous potential of industrial manufacturing, a "bargain between art and labour" leading not only to an impoverished process of production but also to a "makeshift" object. Given that there are other options, Morris asks why the artist and the art lover alike are a "slave to machinery," answering, "because he is the slave to the system for whose existence the invention of machinery was necessary."

Lily and Pomegranate currently circulates as a print, bedspread, wallpaper, sheets, throw-pillow cover, bath curtain, decorative tile, oven mitt, lamp shade, earrings, wine label, picture frame, golf head cover.

Against the cold I wrap my neck with burnt-orange and purple paisley, a five-dollar scarf on offer on almost every Midtown corner but nevertheless reminiscent of luxurious Kashmir shawls. In the Victorian Era some cost as much as a small property and were imported by the East India Company until the United Kingdom began to make her own, patterned with what Europeans named *the paisley* after the Scottish town whose new, mechanical looms mimicked handwoven design at a cheaper price. Mimicked in Scottish wool by Scottish weavers, the *boteh*, the Persian droplet-like motif containing a floral spray combined with a cypress tree—Zoroastrian symbol of life and eternity. The scarves on offer from Manhattan vendors imitate these Scottish imitations and are manufactured in the Global South.

– o — O — o –

In 1886 Freud opens his private practice in Vienna. The Statue of Liberty is dedicated, and Coca-Cola is invented and marketed as a "temperance drink" by Dr. John S. Pemberton, a pharmacist and former colonel of the Confederate Army. Shot and slashed with a sword during battle, Pemberton, who had become addicted to morphine, develops a recipe of cocaine and kola nuts to ease his habit. In 1886 the US Supreme Court rules that corporations have the same rights as living persons. The first gasoline-powered automobile is patented. Spain abolishes slavery in Cuba, and economist Henry George reports that in the US, "Chattel slavery is dead, but industrial slavery remains." After labor unrest and strikes, the eight-hour workday is established. In 1886 the suffrage amendment is defeated in the Senate, two to one. The bustle shrinks and sleeves puff into gigots. The dishwasher is patented. The Martinique house wren and Bennett's seaweed go extinct. The Folies Bergère launches its first music-hall revue, and the last of the eight historic independent Impressionist exhibitions takes place in Paris. Vincent Van Gogh paints *The 14th of July, 1886* and *Head of a Skeleton with a Burning Cigarette*. Robert Louis Stevenson's *Strange Case of Dr. Jekyll and Mr. Hyde* is published. Emily Dickinson and Franz Liszt die. Mary Wigman and Diego Rivera are born. In 1886 Mina Loy, Virginia Woolf, and Melanie Klein are four years old.

– o — O — o –

Four-year-olds sing songs, skip and hop on one foot, walk downstairs alone, draw people with separate body parts, draw circles and squares, and fasten large buttons without help. They may or may not understand the difference between fantasy and reality but realize letters and numbers to be symbols of real things. They have vocabularies between one and two thousand words, which they string together into sentences, questions, and stories. During the Victorian Era some children begin at this age to work on farms, in homes, mines, factories.

Loy is slightly solemn as she poses with her mother, Julia, and two-year-old sister, Dora, for a photograph, circa 1886. She wears a white dress with long sleeves and high collar, her dark hair cropped short as a boy's. Julia stands between the girls, molded into her corset. She turns towards Dora, entirely away from Loy, who gazes at her back. Julia angles one of her arms behind her as if pushing Loy away. Her other arm curves around Dora, whose golden hair curls to her shoulders, the short sleeves of her white dress fluttering like wings.

Little Ova's *wordless / thoughts / grow like visionary plants* in "Anglo-Mongrels and the Rose." Alone in the garden under high skies she realizes *all their / steadfast light is shining out of her.* Light and glass catalyze awareness, and creativity bodies forth via the grotesque when she overhears the phrase *"irraeah"* muttered by the women hovering over her newborn sister's bassinet. *"It is quite green,"* one of them says of Ova's infant sister's runny shit. Too young to know what *"irraeah"* means, Ova freely follows its sound through abstract permutations of color and atmosphere conjuring, it might be argued, her first poem.

At approximately the same age, *Islands in the Air's* Linda creates her first artwork, a sculpture of her baby sister as a feeding bottle made from found objects—a needle, which she wraps around with thread to make *a little tough white belly*. She also takes to turning *round and round until objective reality dissolved* and becomes fascinated by a book, begging to learn how to *decipher the unfamiliar markings*, certain that they contain *the composite brain of humanity.*

I whirl and whirl in the living room until the brown carpet becomes sand and the swimming pool through the sliding glass doors is the aquatic eye of a god who appears and disappears in flashes. I whirl and whirl and whirl until a brown corduroy recliner flings itself into my path. The whirling stops, and my lip splits open, and in this, my first memory, when I wipe my mouth my hand is smeared with the exact same color as my terrycloth dress.

– o — O — o –

Transcribing Loy's manuscripts I write what she writes, draw her language into my body, take it back to the sublet. Infused, the palmette-and-lotus-print curtain finishes with marigold tasseling at the hem. The palmette spiking up speaks. Says "sun" and I am conscious of the sun. The lotus opens, says "womb" and I am conscious of noon ripening. Tassels say "now-now-now" next to the blank white walls which had recently been relieved of their Lincrusta embossed Byzantine and painted to look like leather.

Then the Lincrusta is stripped away, and Mina appears beside me, flesh and blood and whispering into my ear, "The inner life? It is exactly what to many isn't there although it has always been there, prior to birth and exceeding death's picture postcards of bathing girls juxtaposed with limp, flattened, and undulous watches, one of which becomes the saddle of a prostrate animal that seems to be a cross between a seal and a chimera." In contrast, early photography suggests that the real mimics painting; the first railroad cars are designed like stagecoaches; iron is molded into leaves and resembles wood. Industrially produced home goods are shaped into flowers, fauna, seashells or Greek or Renaissance antiquities, and, Terry Eagleton writes, "the years from 1880 to the turn of the century are decades of Tolstoyan simplicitas, and the fellowship of New Life; of the Garden City and rational diet and dress; of a poetry which enacts the essence of the sensuous Object and a philosophy which clings tenuously to the contours of the Real. Europeans had come to occupy and asset-strip the globe."

Arcades of glass, metal, and mirrors enhance the paisley shawl, the beetle wing–strewn dress, and the West is the Roman Emperor Elagabalus as Sir Lawrence Alma-Tadema depicts him in *The Roses of Heliogabalus,* 1888. Gold sheath, gold coronet in his dark hair, lounging on his belly as below him, released upon his command, millions of pink rose petals smother his swooning guests. A cascade against which seeking protection under what is at hand—an enormous ostrich feather fan—is so futile I laugh at the absurdity as I die because I am the Garden City and the string of pearls cultured by surgically wounding each oyster at its sex and placing there a graft from another oyster and a bead of nacre or of resin. Kokichi Mikimoto induces the first such cultured pearl in 1893. Nearly fifty percent of all oysters die or reject their nucleus, even after a century and a quarter of advances. Both natural and artificial pearls yellow and become brittle if not worn. They require the body's heat and oils to keep them luminous.

"Recently," Mina turns to look into the mirror above the mantle, "I see most like a butterfly pinned to augur."

1949

Interlocking inner universes, doves and satellites, sidereal twitching motions one observer points to as possession and another as dance. Yet a third declares the distinction arbitrary for, as Loy writes in her appreciation of Joseph Cornell's 1949 *Aviary* show, *is not the aerial content of a bird partly of the sky?* A chance encounter with caged tropical birds displayed against a pet shop's white walls. The dazzle of magic within a context increasingly weathered.

Sun through the window flares off the mirror. To zip closed the eyes of a seer and deny her hands. She whispers floral vapors in my ear.

– o — O — o –

In 1949 the monkey Albert II is the first primate to survive entry into space. Launched on a US V-2 rocket, he dies when a faulty parachute causes his landing capsule to crash. Set in Allied-occupied Vienna, *The Third Man* wins Cannes Film Festival's Grand Prix. The last sighting of the pink-headed duck is recorded. In 1949 Mao Zedong declares the creation of the People's Republic of China, ending a civil war between the Chinese Communist Party and the

Nationalist Party. The German Democratic Republic is officially established. Radio Free Europe begins broadcasting behind the Iron Curtain. In 1949 Helen Keller, Dorothy Parker, Danny Kaye, Paul Robeson, and other notable Americans are named in an FBI report as Communist Party members. László Rajk, ex-foreign minister of Hungary, accused in a show trial of plotting with Tito to overthrow the Hungarian government and of being a spy for the US, is executed. In 1949 Billy Graham starts the Los Angeles Crusade, his first major evangelical campaign. The first Volkswagen Beetle is sold in the US, and *Hopalong Cassidy*, the first televised western, airs on NBC. Christian Dior's fashions comprise seventy-five percent of Paris's clothing exports and five percent of France's total export revenue. In 1949 the first thing a woman should consider is her silhouette. When named in a war crime trial, Coco Chanel denies accusations that she had been involved with the Nazis. Indonesia, formerly the Dutch East Indies colony, is granted sovereignty from the Netherlands. George Orwell's *Nineteen Eighty-Four* is published. A military coup in Syria ousts the country's democratically elected government. The first Polaroid Camera is sold for $89.95, and Silly Putty costs a dollar. In 1949 Slavoj Žižek, Meryl Streep, Elizabeth Warren, Twiggy, Benjamin Netanyahu, Gil Scott-Heron, and my mother are born. The Julien Levy Gallery closes, and Simone de Beauvoir publishes *The Second Sex*. Anni Albers's solo exhibition at MoMA is the museum's first show dedicated to textiles. The Soviet Union tests its first atomic bomb, RDS-1, otherwise known as Joe. Its design imitates the American plutonium bomb dropped on Nagasaki. The North Atlantic Treaty joins North American and European countries in an intergovernmental military alliance known as NATO. In 1949 *Life* publishes "Jackson Pollock: Is He the Greatest Living Painter in the US?" Canvas on the ground, paint dripping from a brush pulled straight from a can. Robert Motherwell invents the term "New York School," and the Eighth Street Club is formed for private, informal gatherings of artists. Elaine de Kooning and John Cage are early members, although one of the two original unwritten rules is "no women, communists, and homosexuals." It is still 1949.

Loy lives between the East Village and the Bowery in a communal household headed by Klemp, the mother of one of Fabi's friends. Evicted, they move south to an old townhouse at 5 Stanton Street. Definitively the Bowery, definitively skid row, the house has eight rooms, each with a fireplace. Loy fills her rooms with egg crates, rags, bottles, boxes, banana peels, tin cans, clothespins, and other trash from the street. Out of this she fashions three-dimensional collages, constructions, assemblages—her *refusées*. Her writing focuses on the outcast, the derelict, on poverty, and on the spirit. She is greatly moved by Joel Goldsmith's book of spiritual healing, *The Infinite Way*—its revelation that what we seem to seek is ever-present within us, already manifested, and that we need to know this truth. Having generated a series of potentially commercial inventions and designs in the early '40s, never produced, Loy seems now to have dedicated herself solely to art. She and Klemp "darling" each other, and she gets on well with the young acting student and the artist who are her fellow boarders. When Djuna Barnes or Frances Steloff or James Laughlin, Berenice Abbott, Marcel Duchamp, Sidney Janis, or Joseph Cornell visit, Loy hosts them in the common area because her rooms, overflowing with materials, are unsuitable for guests. She befriends the neighborhood's shopkeepers, chatting with them in Italian, and also the homeless to whom she gives money and, following her lifelong compassion for the outcast, kindness. She attempts to publish part of her Book. She wears exclusively deep wine red. Her housemates suspect she dyes her undergarments in the bathroom.

Refusée.

—use, reuse, refuse, fees, sue, ruse, frees, us, fur, see, sere, seer—

– o — O — o –

A new yet primary gesture enters Mina's right arm, sweeping out from the shoulder and then drawing in via fingertips towards her heart. Trailing down her torso to rest on her hip, elbow angled. Her left hand remains tucked in her pocket. Most mornings she performs this primary gesture as she leaves her apartment, careful to step around the sidewalk sleepers, looking into each face for her friend László. When she finds him she wakes him as if accidentally, and they pretend to have not previously met as they carry on in German mixed with pidgin English and Hungarian. He dusts off his clothes as they walk to the lunch counter where she pays for their breakfast. An onion omelet is 25 cents. Soup and coffee is 10. This mutual game of nonrecognition allows his sidewalk sleeping, his filth, his alcoholic stench to be accidental rather than habitual and sets a network of potential universes ashiver such that next time he wakes he recognizes her as an acquaintance he'd last seen in Budapest, 1944, as she was marched by the Arrow Cross men with the other women down Wesselényi Street. Destination: Auschwitz-Birkenau. Slowly stirring cubes of sugar into his coffee, he confides that during Budapest's siege he met a man called Colossus who'd pressed into his hand a letter before valiantly giving his life.

Where did that letter go, dear Mina, dear csíllagom, angyalom, arany virágszál?

Silver sprayed onto the glass's back makes a mirror. The diamond stylus at the tone arm's end makes music. A self-portrait from this time is Cornell's *Aviary* show. Twenty-six distressed white boxes contain cutout birds, carefully mounted mirrors, springs, sets of drawers. Another self-portrait is Dorothea Tanning's 1949 drawing *On Fire*. A breathless, fleeing girl with button boots, Victorian dress, and long hair in flames. Her arms extend into a brick wall through which she hopes to vanish. On the other side she'll find herself as the artist in a red-checked house dress, posed before a bomb shelter, wearing a gas mask. The rubber intoxicates, nauseates, and unlike the Sphinx nuzzling her captors, she refuses to tell Oedipus the answer to her riddle.

Mina had often thought herself to be a form of glass. Refractory, illuminated by the sun. A broken windowpane, cheap lily finial, apothecary bottle transmuted into divine revelation. Light flicks the surface releasing a babble of tongues. Sixty-seven-year-old Loy dressed in wine red and rummaging through trash had always sided with the outcast, the marginal. In *Islands in the Air* Linda would *nurse* her left-hand side in her *astral arms like a doll, croon to it and make ugly faces on its behalf at the aristocratic right.*

Mina leans close to László, catching their image in the mirror behind the lunch counter. Mother and son. Some Blanche with her gigolo. Musk, lemon rind, and gasoline. A dash of sugar spills across a checked cloth.

– o — O — o –

In the archive I find a draft of Loy's meditation on the state of contemporary art and Cornell's *Aviary* show, signed *Mina Loy, 25th of November 1950*. Titled "Phenomenon in American Art," six typescript pages are followed by another five handwritten and numbered to indicate that they directly follow. Accompanying this sequence are two fragments, one of which describes the *degeneration . . . of abstractionism in the gory spatter pictures* that resemble *congealing animal tissue* now so popular that she had recently seen a young artist in his Bowery studio making imitations from photos published in the newspaper. This Loy compares with Brâncuși's *pure abstraction*. The sublime has fallen out of favor because it is not entertaining, and contemporary audiences must be entertained. As such, Cornell's work is essential, for *we are for the first time served sublime entertainment in lieu of "awe."* He opens space for a future at a time when science has used nature as a *medium for smashing creation* and has *reduced the future to hypothesis*. Portions of the essay are excerpted in Loy's 1982 collected, but her larger art-historical argument and social critique remains unpublished.

In 1949 the Surrealist mannequin wakes to find herself corseted into a Christian Dior New Look dress and installed in the American suburbs. She has somehow survived the Depression, the war, and the postwar shortages with her looks intact and is now bent on improving them via the Du Barry Success School's six-week correspondence course—a daily exercise, diet, and cosmetic regimen sent directly to her home accompanied by a complimentary Beauty Case stocked with Du Barry cosmetics. Du Barry Cleansing Cream, Special Cleansing Preparation, Skin Freshener, Lubricating Cream, Derma-Sec Formula, Hand Beauty Cream, Rose Cream Mask, Eye Cream, Foundation Lotion, Cream Rouge, Face Powder, Lip Rouge, Eye Shadow, Lash Beauty, Make-Up Base, Dainty Dry, Creme Shampoo, Creme Rinse, Creme Hair Dressing, Dandruff Treatment.

Having renounced corsets at the turn of the century, having liberated her legs from long skirts by the 1920s, having embraced the trouser, the utility dress, the elegance of well-crafted yet economical lines easily sewn up at home, whatever would possess her to submit to a restricted shoulder, raised bustline, wasp waist contingent on extensive rubber girdling, in-sewn whalebone corsetry, and a skirt so voluminous only a highly trained seamstress might pleat the thirteen-and-a-half yards of fabric into the twelve-inch waist of a gown that requires a maid to attend its complexity?

What forms of consciousness, of creative spirit, does such architecture make possible? Impossible? What forms of desire? The first general charge credit card was conceived in 1950 when a Diners Club cofounder left his wallet in another suit and his wife had to pay the tab. They began with sidecars and ended with bananas Foster and Mrs. So-and-So was resplendent in pearls and blush satin, décolletage scented with White Shoulders's African orange flowers, peaches, and bergamot. She said something unforgivably witty as she took her calfskin wallet from her patent leather purse. Not until 1974 will Mrs. So-and-So be able to apply for credit cards without the signature of her spouse—required regardless of marital status. Control and convenience often share a dress.

Fabric, line, language, gesture aren't solely surface properties because what I am is god and thus the body god, the pleating and stitching god, the milling and spinning god. God the cotton pushing up from earth. God the silkworm. But also then perhaps god the factory, god the landfill, god the click and cart and purchase.

Revealed upon the Italian couturier Mariano Fortuny's death in 1949: Henriette Negrin Fortuny, his wife and muse, invented his renowned pleating technique and designed the iconic 1909 Delphos gown for which he had been famous.

Alan Turing tells *The London Times* in 1949, "I do not see why it [the machine] should not enter any one of the fields normally covered by the human intellect, and eventually compete on equal terms. I do not think you even draw the line about sonnets, though the comparison is perhaps a little bit unfair because a sonnet written by a machine will be better appreciated by another machine." The following year he will introduce "the imitation game," later known as "The Turing Test," a method for determining a machine's ability to exhibit human-like intelligence.

– o — O — o –

To describe 5 Stanton Street as an "old townhouse" conjures grandeur. To date it to the Victorian period entices the imagination with the ornamental flourishes adorning the half-double at 68 Compayne Gardens in Hampstead where Loy's family moved when she was ten, in 1892. Google Maps shows the London street preserved in sunlight—identical three-story brick buildings with pointed roofs, white trimming, bay windows. Wrought iron railings outline terraces on the second and third floors, and short hedges border each property's small front yard. Nearly identical. Entirely tidy. Rubbish-free.

A photo of 5 Stanton Street from the 1940s shows a three-story brick structure with frugal adornment. Slender wedges of pale stone trim the three sash windows of each floor. Paint or grime clouds the front door's transom glass.

Detail is adoration. A tin can, relieved of its wrapper, crushed beyond circumference, rusted out of holding, is secured—but how—to a piece of cardboard rubbed with pastel to an impossible blue.

Filling the front of the invitation card announcing the Bodley Gallery's 1959 exhibition of Loy's *refusées* is Berenice Abbott's black-and-white photograph of *No Parking*, ca. 1950. Against a slatted fence two figures lean or sleep, one draped over a trashcan out of which emerges a butterfly made from a paper cup. The other figure slouches on the ground, surrounded by smashed tin cans, banana peels, frayed rope—a mop head or yarn. The figure's hair is perhaps human, perhaps unanchored from a wig, impossible to tell by the scan of the photograph, its details further blurred by the invitation's textured paper. *No Parking*'s figures are equally feminine and masculine. Their chiseled faces have Loy's wide cheekbones, aristocratic brow. Now lost.

Dramatically different in scale and immediate impression, *No Parking*'s themes and composition—wheel of life, cycle of becoming and unbecoming—nevertheless recall Loy's 1906 gouache and graphite *La maison en paper* featuring six elongated figures caught in a circular progression. At the top is an abstract humanoid shape of incipient form. At the three o'clock position the figure is nude, androgynous. Just after six she holds a rose and wears a violet dress with billowing sleeves and blue tassels. At nine she's aged, stands in profile, her hands clasped in prayer.

When the 5 Stanton Street household is evicted in 1953, rooms are found across the street for Loy and the other boarders although there is no kitchen, no communal area. Her completed *refusées* and materials are moved, piece by piece, by her housemates, but Loy, brought to live in Aspen by her daughters, will never return to New York. Silent under plastic tarping, dust thickening, the artworks await her return, banana peels and eggshells rotting. Compared with Cornell's contemporaneous marbles, mirrors, twigs, dolls, paper palaces, and glass, Loy's work indicates an absolute disregard for longevity. For preservation.

Another Abbott photo captures a small rectangular construction nailed to the wall near Loy's door. A block of wood or a matchbox wrapped in metallic paper. Three cutouts top to bottom reveal a plaster eye, plaster ear, plaster lips. See no evil, hear no evil, speak no evil—a Shinto maxim carved above a temple door in the form of three monkeys covering eyes, ears, mouth. Reminder of god in the eye in the ear in the mouth.

Oak or linden, not matchboxes and cardboard, serve as the traditional icon's foundational panel, covered with linen soaked in isinglass made from air bladders of Russian beluga sturgeon found in the Caspian and Black Seas. Then, a layer of glue and chalk. Onto this the image is inscribed with a needle. Then filled with mineral pigments—cinnabar for reds, iron oxide for yellows, lapis lazuli for blues—mixed with water and yolk and varnished with boiled linseed oil and amber. Made, therefore, from trees, cotton, fish, earth, seed, egg, water. Time-based, eventually rotted things found or harvested or given, but as in Loy's practice, rarely purchased. Transmuted to a figure kept in a wood-heated church or the candle-lit corner of a room. When the image darkens, its caretaker gently rubs alcohol across its surface, then sets it on fire to burn the varnish off.

Refusée.

Refugees. Refusal, refuge, refuse.

A word that sounds artistic, rarified, and French, conferring both irony and dignity upon its figures. In *Christ on a Clothesline*, ca. 1949, a Duchamp-looking paper face drawn to accentuate chiseled cheekbones and a sharp chin is pinned with actual clothespins to a piece of string. Also pinned to the line are a pair of long paper arms, palms out, icon-like. Floating below the face some sort of material—rag, pillowcase, curtain—creates a ghost dress, ghost body. Behind the figure, Loy has constructed out of cardboard a cityscape palimpsest of skyscraper, brick wall, and warehouse.

Figuration invites breathing into the absolute stranger who manifests as a beggar blocking the path. A person nameless unless recognized—or misrecognized—as someone's lost László. What is not understood saturates as spiritual essence, electric blue. The scintillation of flattened tin cans and rags collected on a plot of dirt that had once held flowers. In a red satin slip and wool coat, slowly walking the block while collecting the discarded. To do this unashamed and in the middle of the day until the inner god converses with the discarded's inner god, a netting of lively veins, a webbing of strong muscles.

The Bodley show sells several constructions, priced at $2,000 each, but the majority come to be stored in Levy's Connecticut barn. *Househunting*, ca. 1950, once hung in the pink bedroom of Peggy Guggenheim's Venice palazzo and was later recovered from a storage unit and restored by Carolyn Burke. A cardboard bust of a woman with sheaves of wheat pinned to her breasts balances an elaborate basket on her head containing a ball of yarn and knitting needles, a paper teapot, and a ladder up to a platform over which a clothesline with shirt and pants float. The figure is backed by a large moon—saint's metallic disk. Ten miniature architectural structures radiate around the woman.

Cutting each structure out of paper, lacework of stone and windows tracing London suburb to Munich to London suburb to Paris to Florence to New York to Mexico City to Buenos Aires to Surrey to Geneva to Florence to New York to Paris to Florence to Vienna to Potsdam to Berlin to Florence to Paris to New York to Aspen.

Halo, nimbus, aureole, gloriole, mandorla, circular glow or flames surrounding the head or entire body. By the second-century CE, the halo appears broadly—in Tunisia, Turkey, Pakistan. A few hundred years later it has permeated Christian and Buddhist art.

As if magnetized: float, hover, curl. The body makes its own spiral, its own shell. How else discover the belly of a word but by awakening perceptual capacities toward regenerative metabolism?

I board a 6 a.m. train that will sweep me from New Haven to Grand Central Terminal, then the subway to the Bowery. Passengers nod off, and across their dreaming foreheads the word *refusées* appears. Mina keeps to herself the knowledge of her false teeth, what arid air does to skin. A pinch of sugar and lemon juice to exfoliate. Around the eyes: Vaseline. I made myself all parchment, then remade myself in latex and stretched myself thin as a balloon. Having hovered, it takes an element of hunger to know hunger. It takes an allegiance to ideological blue. The passengers are puzzle creatures with recommendations blooming at the bottom of the screen for the word that will complete the sentence. Refugee. Refuge. From *re* and *fugitive*. Harbor for one who has run away. Refuse—decline, deny. Refuse—matter thrown away.

Tomorrow I'll visit the Whitney for Beatrice Wood's 1976 recreation of her *Un peut (peu) d'eau dans du savon*—original exhibited with Loy's *Making Lampshades* at the April 1917 Society of Independent Artists show and like Loy's painting, like *Fountain*, now lost. Out the Whitney's double-height windows, the sun will strike the Hudson River's surface. Celestial blue despite General Electric dumping between 1947 and 1977 an estimated 1.3 million pounds of PCBs from its plants in Fort Edwards and Hudson Falls. PCBs perhaps at first seemed innocuous, nearly invisible, clear to yellow in color with no smell or taste. They are used widely until skin lesions, liver damage, and in animals given high doses—cancer. Spilled, leaking, and improperly disposed, PCBs have bound themselves with soil and sediment and persist in humans, water, and wildlife as far south as New York Harbor.

After Harlem-125th the train descends underground. In the dark I become aware of a violet buried in my brain, then pushing out. This happens regularly, the violet, the pushing, and sometimes I notice and sometimes I go about locking the sublet's door, making my way to the Beinecke, performing the usual gestures of professional culture, wiping the tears from the corners of my eyes. "What cold weather," I remark to the security guard. The shift at the end of the sentence had once been a pear, a fragrance rushing sensation into the mouth. Inventing oneself out of what is at one's disposal. The crumpled chip bag, the old newspaper, discarded water bottles, face masks collecting along the fence of the parking lot that once had been Loy's 5 Stanton Street residence. Unhomed, the movableness of the I, its lacy, fictive nature longing for Mina in her wine-red coat and hat watching a girl in blue scatter a flock of pigeons.

1936

Fabric cut on the bias at 45 degrees against the weave creates a fluid, body-skimming garment flaring soft at the ankles and balanced by an exaggerated shoulder as in the dress Joan Crawford wears in *Letty Lynton*. Designed by Adrian, diaphanous white organdie with immense ruffled sleeves produces slimming at the hips, a satisfying line which by 1936 makes its way into the design of the suit and simple house dress. In addition to child-sized hips, ruffles fashion an aura of innocence, as if the decade's deepening economic depression and fascism don't exist. A material and ideological *as if* underlying mass-produced patterns. A thousand-franc dress made up for less than fifty.

When Loy writes *Insel*'s Mrs. Jones out the door for a dress fitting, does she mean she's been all-night sewing? The tailor's daughter floats up the stairs—

The beruffled Letty Lynton is most appropriate for the under-twenty-five set, but the bias-cut flatters both twenty and above, commanding the marketplace directly after Madeleine Vionnet's first collection in 1907, shown without corsets or shoes.

Born in 1876, by age twelve Vionnet was apprenticed to a lacemaker, then learned dressmaking from a tailor who specialized in spin-offs of French fashion for the English court. She developed not only the bias cut and Grecian drapery look but also the honeycomb dress, the handkerchief dress, the hemstitched blouse, the halter dress. An early innovator of prêt-à-porter, Vionnet introduced authenticated labels featuring her signature and the imprint of her right thumb. She shuttered her business at the onset of the Second World War, donating most of her designs to the Louvre's Musée de la mode et du textile.

Vogue's photographer captures the undulating folds of Vionnet's 1936 *Winged Victory of Samothrace*–inspired dress as if its draping is swept by a celestial wind. The model poses on a slanted board covered in black fabric, gown pinned against the background.

– o — O — o –

Twenty-one-year-old Julien Levy, fresh out of Harvard and eager to join *les années folles*, arrives in Paris in 1927. To make films. To play a little chess with Duchamp. To Le Dôme and Chez Bricktop. Without delay he befriends Loy and falls in love with nineteen-year-old Joella. They quickly marry and depart for Manhattan where he works for his father's real estate business until his mother's death and subsequent inheritance affords a gallery on Madison Avenue in 1931. Famed for mounting New York City's first show of Surrealism in 1932, Levy's success and the movement of Surrealist art across the Atlantic owe Loy a significant debt.

Studio visits. Gallery openings. Loy scouts, commissions, selects, and contracts work by Giorgio de Chirico, René Magritte, Richard Oelze, Salvador Dalí, and others—many of whom appear in *Insel*. She also stores, crates, and ships pieces to the gallery, and if they return unsold she delivers them back to the artists. Crucially, she ensures the artists are paid, often lobbying Levy to give the struggling a show, paying what the gallery owes out of her own small account, reimbursing herself when the money finally arrives. Her letters to Levy held in his papers at the Philadelphia Museum of Art reveal not only labor, but investment—creative, intellectual, physical. A 1934 Dalí returns damaged, and she gives it the *touch of vernis à retoucher* that it needs. When a 1935 Dalí comes back, she discovers that a *piece of the lion's head which had been glued on had come off*. The canvas also has a hole in the center which, within a week, she repairs.

– o — O — o –

No more boning, no more rubber, no more elastic suturing the real to the surreal to the irreal to the infra-real. By 1936 home, if ever Loy would call any place home, is an apartment in Djuna Barnes's building at 9 rue St.-Romain where she and Fabi have moved so as to be less lonely after Joella's departure. So as to own something against future's increasing insecurity. O light-flooded entrance hall furnished with flea market metal dining room chairs painted lemon, sky, petal. Scuffed parquet floors, tall ceilings, milk-glass chandeliers.

Google Maps–walking rue St. Romain in Montparnasse it's all ashlar facing until no. 9, brick-clad above the ground floor and beveling around a courtyard fronted by a wrought-iron fence. Six stories of French doors with balconies fitted out with planter boxes commune companionably. Date-stamped May 2019. The geraniums begin to bloom. It's an eleven-minute walk to Gertrude Stein's. Twenty-three to Natalie Barney's. Le Dôme, La Rotonde, Le Select, La Coupole, and Hôtel Lutetia—just eleven. The arrondissement on a Sunday is pristine, shuttered, quiet, the only human presence a blurred figure searching for an open internet café. An eternal present until the data change.

Meilleursagents.com allows entrance into a no. 9 unit renovated to accommodate twenty-first-century convenience while losing none of its honeyed herringbone parquet, high ceilings, white walls, and crown moldings. Voile drapes open, French doors open to reveal the bright gash of geraniums. The price exceeds a million Euros. In 1936 Mina steps onto her balcony, and across the courtyard Djuna appears.

I stand at the open French doors to catch a small breeze. Hemmed with white tassels and silver bells, the curtains jangle, feathery. The apartment's an island, the private island of writing equipped with a private dock, private landing strip, all access points patrolled by a private security force. Not even I know what's tucked in this inner recess, deepest recess, labyrinth leading to bosom, sacred heart, solar plexus, guts.

In 1936, silver paper arranged in floral patterns across the walls conceals crumbled plaster. Squares of colored cellophane cover the sitting room's glass doors, and light splays from the chandelier above a small round table. Plinth for the *Lobster Boy,* ca. 1930, floating in a bell jar. A humanoid figure with breasts, lobster tail instead of legs, claws in place of arms. My eyes burn like two dark coals. A garland of wire roses tightens around my brow as I look out from the aquarium.

Submerged, where does the mind end and the book begin? Where does skin end and water begin? Amniotic floating I meet Dora Maar, Meret Oppenheim, and Pablo Picasso at the back of the Café de Flore. Mirrors stud mahogany paneling, multiply Picasso's Breton jersey and Oppenheim in liquid gold. Vacances, a 1936 green-floral perfume by Jean Patou conjures the flowers, fruit, and grass of the first paid holidays in France—courtesy of the newly elected Popular Front.

Maar caresses the ocelot fur that wraps the brass tubing Oppenheim has converted to a bracelet. Picasso murmurs, "tu peux tout couvrir de fourrure" as Oppenheim holds her teacup to the waiter. She thinks, "mehr Fell bitte" but says, "un peu plus de fourrure," and he fills her cup with a bow. Maar brushes the blonde wave of her hair from her eyes. A painting might not evoke the sensation of fur, but a photograph can, yes it can, yes it can. Furred, but don't touch! With a continuous gesture Oppenheim rests cup to saucer and departs for the Uniprix department store to purchase the demitasse and spoon she'll cover with the fur of a Chinese gazelle.

As Oppenheim pastes fur to bone china, she cries. Not big-stuttering-gulps-of-air cries, but you-wouldn't-have-known-she-was-crying-but-for-the-perfect-single-crystal-droplet-slowing-down-her-cheek cries. She cries not on behalf of herself, but on behalf of mein Vater barred in Germany from practicing psychoanalysis by the 1935 Nuremberg Race Laws. No longer able to send to Paris the usual monthly sum.

The Modern Woman had been a sleek machine, but by 1936 she's disassembled into a baroque-framed mirror held by a statue's severed hand reflecting a blank sky, full moon. Then the same mirror, held by a woman's hand, reveals a blonde bombshell in a white scalloped dress. Hair caressed with pomade, she lifts a mask painted with her own features. Plucked brows, Revlon mouth, tongue furred.

In 1936 the last Tasmanian tiger dies in Tasmania's Beaumaris Zoo. Hitler occupies the Rhineland in direct violation of the Treaty of Versailles, and the Gestapo is placed above the law. Germany hosts the winter and summer Olympics, and the Roma, the homeless, and other "undesirables" are sent to concentration camps guarded by the newly formed SS *Totenkopf* Death's Head division. Jesse Owens wins four gold medals. In 1936 Italy annexes Ethiopia and proclaims the King of Italy its emperor. Upon the capture of Addis Ababa, Il Duce announces the foundation of the New Roman Empire. In 1936 the Spanish Civil War begins. Federico García Lorca is arrested in Granada and shot by a firing squad. The Queen Mary begins Atlantic crossings and is nicknamed "The Ship of Woods" for its marquetry, carvings, and murals done in fifty-six veneers—one for each protectorate of the British Empire. Six of these woods are now extinct, a fact I don't know when I am sixteen and perform Anna Pavlova's *Dying Swan* in its rented-out ballroom—ship permanently moored in Southern California since 1967. King Edward VIII abdicates the British throne to marry American divorcée Wallis Simpson. His brother King George VI will see the United Kingdom through the War. He will be the last Emperor of India—British Raj dissolved in 1947. The Hoover Dam is finished, the first radioactive substance is produced synthetically, and the first X-ray photo of arterial circulation is made in Rochester, New York. In 1936 the Crystal Palace, built in Hyde Park to house the Great Exhibition of 1851, is destroyed by fire. Walter Benjamin's "Das Kunstwerk im Zeitalter seiner technischen Reproduzierbarkeit," published the previous year, is translated and published in French. Eva Hesse, Carolee Schneemann, Mary Tyler Moore, and Robert Redford are born. Rudyard Kipling, Maxim Gorky, and Ivan Pavlov die. Sunscreen, the helicopter, and the Zippo lighter are invented, and Jacques Lacan makes his first presentation of his theory of the "mirror stage." In the US unemployment nears 17 percent, and there are over two thousand strikes, mainly in the textile, construction, and transportation industries. The BBC begins its first regular public television broadcasts, and a November 1936

Harper's Bazaar article claims, "This Year is the Surrealist's Year," interviewing Julien Levy because "nobody in America knows more about Surrealism than he does."

"By 'corpse,'" Mina says through the apartment's dusk as she bends over the typewriter, "we mean both flesh and context. The body of the dead—Colossus, Giles, Oda Janet, Father, Mother—our own mortal form as well as the constellation of forces that hold the body to the living." Just as a cube in the zeroth dimension manifests as a single point, the third dimension traces just one single aspect. Loy channels a greater reality through Insel, the character she models after the German Expressionist Richard Oelze who paints *Expectation* in 1935, acquired, via Loy, by Levy the following year and purchased by MoMA in 1940. In blues and greens and browns and grays a crowd of men and a few women stand with their backs to the viewer. They face into the distance under a punishing sky. Insel, German for "island," in early drafts was named *Totenkopf*. Skull and bones.

Mrs. Jones, like Loy, is an expatriate writer, artist, and the Paris agent for an American art gallery. Upon meeting Insel she's captivated by his *Strahlen*—magnetic connectivity that alters the atmosphere, heals *the lightning hand of pain.* Truth body, astral body, Dharmakāya, vibration body. Whatever one in the third dimension is, is partial. Loy writes to Levy of sitting outside at the Hôtel Lutetia's café with Man Ray and Oelze. As air raid sirens roar, she's overwhelmed by a strong feeling that *some effort should be made* on Oelze's behalf. Can Levy ask Alfred Barr to find someone to sponsor his immigration to America? *The volcano is about to Europe-Erupt.*

Strahlen enthrals—*Strahlen* enthrals—*Strahlen* enthrals—

Mrs. Jones's body, Insel's body, *Insel's* body, the body of Loy's Book metamorphoses into a balloon. The arms are two ribbons of electricity. The ribcage is the Eiffel Tower and flowing from the womb: the Seine. Factories puff away on the riverbank, and the heart is a wandering Chinese gazelle amazed she still exists, bereft, as she is, of her pelt. To starve until becoming nothing more than *Strahlen* prisming the wall.

This body dispersed contrasts with the unified body proposed by *Olympia,* Leni Riefenstahl's documentary film of the 1936 Olympic Summer Games. Her camera sweeps across ruins on the Acropolis, then slows over several ancient sculptures until finding the Discobolus by Myron. Nude, the sculpture glistens and then dissolves. In its place stands Erwin Huber, fulfilling Hitler's ideal, "quick as a greyhound, tough as leather, hard as Krupp steel." Restless, Loy foresees a young Discobolus reclining on her bed. He effaces the slight depression left where Insel had been sleeping. It is then she knows: German tanks will parade down the Champs-Élysées as troops scale the Eiffel Tower in a war exercise. The premonition of the soldier—a mere boy—has been delivered by the plaster ceiling's cracks.

To foresee requires understanding the eye to be dependent not only on the retina, optical nerve, and lens, but on elements that might be disregarded as almost nothing at all. The vitreous humor—a clear, firm, jelly-like substance composed of 99 percent water, 1 percent collagen, protein, salts, sugars—maintains the eye's shape and lets in light.

Given Hitler's expanding power, Loy sends Fabi to live with Joella and Julien, and in 1936 sells her apartment at a loss, moving to New York City, never to see Europe again. *The self is a decomposition of the whole—the whole—the composite origin of our experience*

Loy scrawls on a scrap of paper. *Let us meditate on the nature of our experience.*

The meat-self in 1936 is uncorseted and lounges in the back of a jazz club on a velvet divan. Is the athletic New Woman. Is barefoot modern dancers and German *Nacktkultur*'s nudists frolicking in meadows. Bodies of meat, manes of grass, eyes of glass, and every given thing has a face. Even as she poses for *Weeping Woman* in Picasso's studio, Maar radiates her own photographic images of embryonic animals, clay figures, fur masks. A blind man holds out a begging bowl. Shadows, chandeliers, a swimming pool striated with light. Among the objects Maar documents at the 1936 *Exposition surréaliste d'objets* at the Galerie Charles Ratton are Oppenheim's fur teacup, *Object*, and Leonor Fini's *Cover of a Book That Has Spent Time in the Sea,* encrusted with shells and sand and pretending to be Christopher Columbus's logbook. Also, Marcel Jean's *Specter of the Gardenia*, the plaster head of a woman Jean had found at the Marché aux Puces—a copy, he insists, of a portrait of Madame du Barry, Louis XV's last official mistress. Covered in black wool carefully smoothed over her features, she is slightly fuzzy. Zippers over her eyes conceal a tiny photo of a face and a tiny photo of a star. The filmstrip collar around *Specter*'s neck was shot by one of Maar's lovers, and nobody seems to know whether Maar would appear if it were projected. The gardenia was Freud's favorite flower. Water touched to petals turns them brown.

Gemsandladders.com/collection/fur_bracelet offers a reproduction of Oppenheim's bracelet in 18 karat gold, price available upon request. Also on offer: gold versions of Oppenheim's snake ear cuff and sugar cube ring. The wearer can freely exchange the cube for a real gem at any time. Language is a technology that can exceed the limits of a single, three-dimensional position.

Elsa Schiaparelli will purchase the original bracelet from Oppenheim for twelve Swiss francs with rights of manufacture. Or it will be given to Schiaparelli by Picasso, who will have charmed it from Oppenheim. Or it was Alberto Giacometti, who first encouraged Oppenheim to produce fashion accessories and jewelry for Schiaparelli, who will buy the first fur-covered bracelet for about five dollars. Or Oppenheim will give it to Aube Elléoüet, Jacqueline Lamba and André Breton's daughter, born in 1935. Baby Aube gumming fur and cooing. Lamba securing the bracelet in a jewelry chest she tucks into a cardboard box labeled *Dawn*. "Si tu me quittes, je te détruirai," replies Breton to Lamba's request for a divorce. Spiraling organic forms, earth tones massaged into silvers, coppers, golds—the paintings Lamba makes from 1935 until the war and leaves at the Paris apartment where she and Breton have lived until they flee will never be recovered.

– o — O — o –

A woman sits just inside her canvas shelter, baby on her lap. Two of her children, faces turned from the camera, lean against her shoulders. She draws her right hand to her chin, chiseled Cherokee features, and gazes at the impossible distance. "I saw and approached the hungry and desperate mother," Dorothea Lange will later say, "as if drawn by a magnet." The family survives on frozen field vegetables and birds the children kill with stones—so says the story, later countered by the family. Not scavengers, they worked twelve-hour days in the fields for food. "I didn't," Lange will later say, "catch her name." The original print will have the tip of Lange's finger in the shot. Captioned by the Library of Congress

"Destitute pea pickers in California. Mother of seven children. Age thirty-two. Nipomo, California," 1936.

Journalists trace Florence Owens Thompson to a trailer park in Modesto, California, nearly forty years later. Produced while Lange was employed by the US government's Farm Security Administration, *Migrant Mother* has always been in the public domain. Lange does not, therefore, earn royalties, and Thompson receives no compensation for being the face of Depression-era American poverty circulating as t-shirt, tote bag, poster, bath mat, fleece blanket, throw pillow, coffee mug.

Postcards of *Object* and *Migrant Mother* are propped against the sublet's desk lamp. *Object* made its American debut at MoMA's 1936 Surrealist exhibition. When Barr proposed the museum acquire the piece for its collection, the board declined. He purchased it himself from Oppenheim for fifty dollars—half her asking price. The event of being is furred and wet as you drink from the cup. Also dry in the mouth: locusts devouring fields. At last count, only an estimated 350 Chinese gazelles remain.

Even in the form of postcards, *Object* and *Migrant Mother* transmit rays.

In 1936 "Polaroid," "nightspot," and "cathect" enter the lexicon. In 2024 dora-maar.com is "the only marketplace where you can shop luxury fashion from your favorite Muses." Chanel, Dior, Fendi, Gucci, Prada, Valentino, etcetera. Extra 40 percent off sale items, 30 percent off full price.

– o — O — o –

The smoking room is pressurized with a swivel air lock to prevent leaking hydrogen. Clouds and the Atlantic and some of the islands of the Azores sweep by. The menu is tenderloin steak and beans *à la princesse*. A silver shell four times longer than the Boeing 747 will be. A propaganda tool for Nazi Germany with five Olympic rings celebrating the Berlin games on its hull, swastika on its company flag, h-i-n-d-e-n-b-u-r-g lettered in red Fraktur script. The airship tours Germany dropping leaflets in support of occupation of the Rhineland in violation of the Treaty of Versailles before embarking on the first of its seventeen commercial transatlantic flights in 1936. In October, the all-male millionaires' flight, a ten-and-a-half-hour cruise over New England, carries Nelson Rockefeller, US and German government and military officials, the CEOs of Eastern Airlines, TWA, and Pan American. Stewards carefully pack the passengers' hand luggage with souvenir silver ashtrays featuring glass models of the airship filled with ESSO diesel fuel.

On the other side of a café, a theater, a salon, someone wears a Schiaparelli hat shaped like a shoe, and Mina daubs Shocking's rose behind her ears. Someone wears an evening dress printed with lobsters and parsley, cummerbund of coral silk. I wear mother-of-pearl buttons engraved with tiny footprints and change my name, but my responses to even the simplest questions remain opaque. As if answering for all, Dalí begins wearing his famed diver's suit, a jeweled sword at his side, accompanied by two borzoi dogs on a leash. Loy keeps his 1931 *Persistence of Memory* in her apartment before crating it for Levy. How many hours of her life—thousands? more?—does she spend taking inventory and packing fragile objects—lamps, hats, paintings, sculpture—to be shipped here and there across seas and continents?

Dalí paints Joella's hair and neck orange, extends this across the right side of her plaster bust, adding a brick motif. He paints the left side with a landscape of sky and elongated clouds, which also appear through a hole in the brick wall of her right cheek. This brick wall, its failure to conceal an ever-shifting sky, is this what Loy means when, not long before her death on September 25, 1966, she takes Joella's hand, kisses it, and whispers *I never knew what you were?* The outline of Dalí's sculpture, when seen from afar, is that of a violin.

Late at night I care less about the melting clocks than about the poor biomorphic form, part-profile, part sea-creature, long lashes insinuating the tenderness of pincushions and dreams.

Magazines report that for your coat the newest fabric looks harsh and rough to the eye but has a pleasantly soft texture. I therefore make up my face to look harsh to the eye but wear my satin chamise. The exterior comes in the conventional black or blue and in marvelous neutral mixtures. It's the old ensemble idea again, nostalgic filter, we've already said our goodbyes. According to Loy's biography, when she arrives in New York in 1936 she looks much older than her fifty-four years.

Moons, comets, teasing a butterfly, coronets, dawn, the bewitched, light, stars, stars, stars.

Joseph Cornell's film *Rose Hobart* premiers at the Julien Levy Gallery in December of 1936. He's removed every scene in the 1931 B-movie *East of Borneo* not featuring Hobart, reassembled the pieces, and spliced them with snippets of other films for a twenty-minute short projected at silent-film speed through a blue-tinted lens. All is nighttime's luminous violet as a small crowd watches an eclipse. The film cuts to the heroine sleeping, gauzed by a mosquito net, candle flickering. Then returns to a shot of the people watching the eclipse, then cuts to a ball falling in slow motion into a pool of water which ripples out. As if part of the magic, Hobart's clothing changes suddenly between shots. Linen safari suit replaced by a beaded dinner gown. She raises an arm, tilts her head. In nearly constant motion, she's nevertheless stopped from exiting the frame.

1897

The protagonist enters her boudoir dressed in a satin ballgown, off-the-shoulder neckline. She waves her hands and moves her mouth to indicate that she is talking-talking-talking as she's followed by her maid helping her unhook as they walk. Dress, petticoat, bloomers, corset, and garters discarded, the protagonist sits in her slip near the low-lipped tin tub. She is still talking-talking-talking as her maid helps her remove her shoes and stockings. Then standing and stepping into the bath, back to us, stripping off her slip to a flesh-colored bodysuit—cinema's first impression of female nudity. As Georges Méliès's 1897 *Après le bal (le tub)* ends, the maid pours a pitcher of water over the protagonist, scrubs her back. The boudoir-backdrop is pinned to the peach orchard's wall of Méliès's family property. The pitcher of water is filled with dark sand to prevent the actress from catching a chill.

– o — O — o –

Mina's wearing a kaftan of gold cranes interlocked with blue stars, hair wrapped in a paisley turban. A padded envelope carrying a half-dozen dresses individually sealed in plastic pouches spills onto the bed. Gem-tone blossoms and lashing vines. Flying creatures from birds to wasps to comets. They're from India and advertised as coming from artisanal workshops, not sweatshops, but one never knows and how can I, but could I?

"One should either be a work of art, or wear a work of art"—so says Oscar Wilde.

Tonight I'm occupied with *The Yellow Book: An Illustrated Quarterly*. Signature goldenrod cover intended to conjure French novels' indecency, and this issue, the last issue, April 1897, has a silhouette of two interlocked roosters on both front and back. A confrontation of talons and beaks, their plumage spirals to the edge of the frame. A cockfight by the unknown Mabel Syrett.

Aubrey Beardsley's voluptuous laughing woman with a beauty mark in a half-mask with an angular, androgynous figure hovering sensuously over her left shoulder launched the magazine three years before. "Hideous," proclaims *The Nation*. Notable only for its "repulsiveness and insolence," hisses *The London Times*. In the series of Salomés that Beardsley draws during this time for the English translation of Wilde's play, Salomé levitates in a white robe, writhing snake-like hair, her face in profile with bee-sting lips, eyes critical slits. She holds up John the Baptist's severed head. Blood drips from his neck, pools into a lily. The English ivy chokes out the tree it climbs, but which is the ivy and which is the tree?

In his original illustration, Beardsley includes a line repeated throughout the play under Salomé's floating body. Spiky, hand-lettered script—"J'ai baisé ta bouche Iokanaan, J'ai baisé." For the published version he simplifies hairline calligraphic flourishes and erases the phrase but retains Salomé's languid, Pre-Raphaelite body and her chiseled face. John the Baptist is celestially androgynous. The first work of British Art Nouveau. A foretaste of Ziggy Stardust.

Wilde's French is imperfect, lines of dialogue unattached to specific characters, and his handwriting adopts the lowercase epsilon and alpha for e's and a's as he composes *Salomé* in Paris. A new language, a new skin, a new sex. The heart-shaped bodice of strapless turquoise satin attached to the three-tiered tulle skirt. Wilde wears a long, tendrilled wig, paste jewels, smooth bare chest and kneels before a platter with John the Baptist's head, photograph undated. The New York Public Library's collection of his papers includes a manuscript forgery of *Salomé*, signed "Oscar Wilde" and thought to have been produced by the hand of Fabian Lloyd, a.k.a. Arthur Cravan.

Cheekbones, nose, and lips sharp as a silver hatchet, Beardsley wears his cropped hair tinted green, favors dove-gray suits, ties, hats, and yellow gloves. After Wilde's trial, conviction, and sentencing to two years of hard labor in Reading Gaol for homosexuality, Beardsley is removed from the masthead of *The Yellow Book*. In prison when *Salomé* is produced in Paris, and five years dead in 1905 when it is produced for private performances in London, Wilde never sees his play performed.

Mina draws a circle on her forehead with gold lipstick, outlines it in red, and surrounds it with rhinestone stars.

A *Gazette des beaux-arts* review describes Loy's 1906 Salon d'Automne work as "strange watercolors where are combined Guy, Rops and Beardsley . . . ambiguous ephebes whose nudity is caressed by ladies in the furbelows of 1885." *Lunar Baedecker* [*sic*] will go out of print almost immediately when it is published in 1923, in part because US customs confiscated literature thought to violate obscenity laws.

– o — O — o –

In 1897 Claude Monet begins the *Water Lilies* series. The word "computer," from the Latin *putare*, to think, to prune, is used to refer not only to a human who performs calculations but also to a calculating machine. J. J. Thomson of the Cavendish Laboratory announces his discovery of the electron as a subatomic particle, and drillers near Bartlesville, Oklahoma, strike oil on land leased from the Osage tribe. In 1897 Bram Stoker's *Dracula* is published in London. During the Bombay epidemic, Ukrainian bacteriologist Waldemar Haffkine performs on himself the first human trial for a vaccine for the bubonic plague. In 1897 123 Black Americans are known to have been lynched. The portable pencil sharpener is patented by American inventor John Lee Love, and the first submarine with an internal combustion engine is demonstrated. In 1897 Queen Victoria celebrates her Diamond Jubilee to mark sixty years on the throne and the British Empire's crown jewels: its colonies. In Assam, an earthquake of magnitude 8.0 kills over 1,500 people. Aubrey Beardsley publishes *A Book of Fifty Drawings*, and in 1897 Havelock Ellis and John Addington Symonds publish *Sexual Inversion*, the first volume of *Studies in the Psychology of Sex*. The Martinique giant rice rat, Nelson's rice rat, and the New Zealand thrush go extinct. In 1897 women are admitted to the École des beaux-arts, whereas the Royal Academy of Art opened its school to women in 1860. In England there are eighty-seven female doctors; in France, ninety-five. Gigot sleeves are at their largest, and instead of dividing the body in half with an hourglass effect, the new corsets push muscle, flesh, and fat upwards for a Pouter pigeon look. In 1897 Martha Graham is three years old. The Moscow Art Theatre is formed by Konstantin Stanislavski and Vladimir Nemirovich-Danchenko. A meteorite enters the Earth's atmosphere and explodes over New Martinsville, West Virginia. In 1897 the Klondike Gold Rush begins. The Tate Gallery opens in England; in France Stéphane Mallarmé publishes *Un coup de dés n'abolira le hasard* in *Cosmopolis: An International Monthly Review*. It will not appear in book form until 1914, sixteen years after his death. In reaction against artistic conservatism, the Vienna

Secession is founded. In her signature black dress, white lace collar, black hat, the sixty-year-old union organizer and activist Mary G. Harris is given the name "Mother Jones" by coal miners calling for a nationwide strike. In 1897 Charles Scott Sherrington introduces the term "synapse," Émile Durkheim publishes *Le suicide,* and Guglielmo Marconi sends the first wireless communication over open sea.

– o — O — o –

On the left—the drawing of a skeleton. On the right—the skeleton as trained by a corset to narrow her rib cage, narrow her solar plexus until she collapses, a small sun, into herself. As a child I considered the figures of my imagination to be my friends, sisters, twins, but by fifteen I consigned them to an ideal of who I wanted to be and called them far planets and all that I was not. Both skeletons have the same life-like head, hair twisted, braided, coiled into a serpentine cap reminiscent of the central figure in *Surreal Scene*, Loy's 1930s peach-toned painting of transforming female forms. Except for red lace-up ankle boots, *Surreal Scene's* central figure is nude, and you can see into her body, posed in the flat, frontal manner of a Byzantine figure. An infinity sign for lips, an hourglass in the place of her nose.

White lilies bloom at each breast; delicate sheathes of wheat rustle at her solar plexus; a glass chalice of wine balances in her abdomen. Standing next to this central figure is a small, dark-skinned girl, also nude, with an upside-down head, large round eyes. A form that draws on racist stereotypes. She shoots stars from the mouth of a musical instrument—part saxophone, part garden hose, part snake—toward a pale hybrid female figure with a unicycle body attached to a green-clad torso and head of streaming red hair. The hybrid woman catches one of the stars in her hands. Above the girl and the bicycle woman, a ribcage hovers, extracted and enlarged like an anatomy illustration. The ribcage contains a heart, liver, entrails, and a miniature embracing couple that evokes Edward Burne-Jones's *Love Among the Ruins*, a favorite of Linda's in *Islands in the Air*.

The granite city surrounding the couple has been destroyed, yet the briar rose and bluebells bloom. Leaning her head on her lover's shoulder, the woman clasps her arms around his neck, her bright blue gown extending into the flowers scattered on the ground. Maria Zambaco, the model for Burne-Jones's female figure, is mainly remembered for having been his mistress and muse. Zambaco inherited a fortune at fifteen, studied painting and drawing at the Slade, and was mentored by Auguste Rodin. She specialized in sculpted medals, taking—instead of famous men—women as her subject, many of them friends. These she exhibited at the Royal Academy, the Arts and Crafts Exhibition Society, and in the Paris Salon. Several are preserved in the British Museum's collection.

Zambaco is relatively free to live as she pleases, although how free is she, married by eighteen to someone eleven years her senior and with two children by twenty-three? The marriage in ruins and returning to live with her mother and then attempting to pry Burne-Jones away from his wife Georgiana, trying, the story goes, to entice him to enter with her into a suicide pact. Georgiana, also an artist, had joined the Pre-Raphaelite circle at fifteen and was influenced by John Ruskin. A painter and engraver, she makes many of the costumes the models wear in the circle's elaborately frocked paintings and was an astonishing embroideress. After Burne-Jones's death she writes a two-volume chronicle of the Pre-Raphaelite movement, *Memorials of Edward Burne-Jones,* still in print via Cambridge University Press. Her 1857 watercolor *Dead Bird*, held at the Tate, presents a life-sized green-headed tanager in such detail it might be mistaken for featherwork.

A sketch of Marianne Moore. A drawing of a woman with red hair. A series of untitled sketches labeled "artist unidentified." The Beinecke's folders of drawings and inventions. Aside from these works, all of Loy's artistic production currently lives outside institutional contexts.

– o — O — o –

Fifteen-year-old Loy stands before a backdrop of misty florals, an urn of daisies at her feet. Flanked by rustic trees scalped of their canopies, she holds a Chinese parasol over her right shoulder, gazes wistfully into the camera, dark hair spilling over the white ruffled bodice of her shirt, plain dark skirt. Suspended in a photo between the form of a girl and the form of a woman, circa 1897, she's just finished her compulsory education, and her parents, uncertain what to do with her, agree to enroll her in St. Johns Wood's Art School.

The brittle *Islands in the Air* typescript recalls the cheap, brown scratch paper of elementary school that ripped under the eraser. Not meant to last. I touch the manuscript as seldom as possible, but the scanned version on my iPad I tap and pull and drag. I stretch the image to enlarge the type, the penciled correction, the delicate sketch. On page 101 the typewriter ink is particularly uneven, and the top left-hand corner has a blotch—perhaps water, perhaps tea. Three penciled dots on a Loy typescript mean "stet," her habit of crossing out paragraphs means, usually, not "discard" as I initially thought but that she's incorporated them into a subsequent draft. Above the lines of type, handwritten words provide variants; for example, here the art teachers are, in ironic scare quotes, *"masters"* crossed-out to *professors*. She works and reworks abstract nouns—*intuition* on this page replaced by *intention*. *Ambition* replaced by *preoccupation*.

Copying busts in the antique room. Praise for fidelity to the contours of the live model. Linda's true education happens in the margins. At tea in the private studio of one of the older students, she hears the headmaster say *all matter is composed of atoms*, and on the floor of the ladies' dressing room she finds a page from a review of Max Nordau's *Degeneration*—a two-volume condemnation of nearly every new current. Oscar Wilde, Henrik Ibsen, Charles Baudelaire, Friedrich Nietzsche, Dante Gabriel Rossetti. The name Dante Gabriel Rossetti smells to Linda like a glorious *pot-pourri*. Tantalized, his poems will prove *so powerful an emetic of the spirit as to relieve a middle-class visionary of her adolescence and clog the gorgeous rubber "crops" of your wide-eyed women stricken with fried hair—*

Mina closes her parasol, shifts her weight, adjusts her hem. René Lalique completes his foot-long Dragonfly Lady corsage pin, affixes the small, green enamel torso modeled after Sarah Bernhardt to a gold creature composed of a long, jointed scorpion tail and a double set of gryphon claws. The enamel woman emerges bare-breasted, unfurling her dragonfly wings. When pinned to a moving, breathing body, her articulated tail and delicate, hinged wings shimmer to life.

The top of the "W" is worn away in many of the manuscript pages Loy typed in Paris in the '20s and '30s. In *Islands in the Air*, written on a New York typewriter in the '40s and '50s, the W is quite clear, but significantly darker, as if Loy's left ring finger came down with added force.

– o — O — o –

Cyclamen, roots, and stems writhe in gold silk on fine blue linen. The "whiplash line" is revealed to Londoners at the 1896 Arts and Crafts exhibition via Hermann Obrist's *coup de fouet* embroidery.

Then travelling abroad and finding the whiplash in the wrought iron railings and ceramic floors of Victor Horta's Hôtel Tassel in Brussels. And in cast iron balustrades and the enormous dipping heads of the Paris Metro's lampposts with their red glass flower-bud insect-eyes. And the hair of the women Alphonse Mucha draws for advertisements of cigarette papers and travel by rail. Monaco to Monte Carlo their hair tendrils and cascades over the bodices of muslin dresses delicately ornamented at the neck, sleeves, and hem with jewel beetle wings arranged in rosettes vined together with gilded thread.

The garments of the eighteenth and nineteenth century court in Jaipur, spectacularly ornamented with elytra—the iridescent casings of jewel beetle wings—enchant England when the East India Company and the British military occupy India. By the 1860s elytra were imported by the shipload to be applied in imitation of the Indian technique.

A whiplash line in gold just under the collarbones.

Carl Van Vechten recalls that Loy wore dresses of "dove-coloured shades, or brilliant lemon with magenta flowers, or pale green and blue . . . extremely lovely. Strange, long earrings dangled from her artificially rosy ears: one amber pair imprisoned flies with extended wings."

"I was reaching," Mina says, looking up from her notebook, face half-shaded by her brim, "more than I was plotting. I was thoroughly on reprieve from decease, a lucid iris of evergreen until the eye, snipped from its socket, becomes an object for inspection held in the hand. Gentle scalpel around the edges to crack it open like an oyster, allowing vision to break loose."

– o — O — o –

Through the glass I press my fingers to paper skin that had been taken by the archivist to the scanner to be infused with light. As never before. Even when held up to the sun.

Light had stricken the document, bouncing off to reflect from mirrors to the scanner lens which directed it to a circuit of sensors that converted levels of brightness into electric signals then processed into digital images.

The duration of a thing is how long it takes to burn out, dissolve, cease to be.

Seated in a carriage a woman wearing a hat bedecked with pink and white flowers leans slightly forward to look out. Framed by the carriage's brown curtains. Her sidelong gaze catches mine. A man in an emerald-green top hat is partially visible next to her. Seated across, a nurse or a peasant woman in white exposes her breast to feed a swaddled infant. Mixed media on paper, circa 1900. One of Loy's earliest known surviving works. The lives of women, social class, the details of materiality, the significance of framing. And of touch. Origin-preoccupations, ongoing.

The Loy-like woman holds a single flower, not yet finished, in her hand.

The sugar dissolves. The window burns.

The document becomes pure light.

Sources

Books by Mina Loy

Lunar Baedecker. Dijon: Contact Publishing Company, 1923.

Lunar Baedeker & Time-Tables. Highlands: Jargon Society, 1958.

The Last Lunar Baedeker. Edited by Roger L. Conover. Highlands: Jargon Society, 1982.

Insel. Edited by Elizabeth Arnold. Santa Rosa: Black Sparrow Press, 1991.

The Lost Lunar Baedeker. Edited by Roger L. Conover. New York: Farrar, Straus and Giroux, 1996.

Stories and Essays of Mina Loy. Edited by Sara Crangle. Champaign: Dalkey Archive Press, 2011.

Insel. Edited with an afterword by Elizabeth Arnold, new material edited with an introduction by Sarah Hayden. Brooklyn: Melville House Publishing, 2014.

Lost Writings: Two Novels by Mina Loy. Edited by Karla Kelsey. New Haven: Yale University Press, 2024.

Fine Press Editions of Mina Loy

At the Door of the House. Northampton: Aphra Press, 1980.

Love Songs. Northampton: Aphra Press, 1981.

Virgins Plus Curtains: Poems by Mina Loy. Rochester: The Press of the Good Mountain, 1981.

Mina Loy Papers

Mina Loy Papers, Yale Collection of American Literature, Beinecke Rare Book and Manuscript Library, Yale University. YCAL MSS 6.

Mina Loy Work and Letters in Other Collections

Carolyn Burke Collection on Mina Loy and Lee Miller, Yale Collection of American Literature, Beinecke Rare Book and Manuscript Library, Yale University. YCAL MSS 788.

Julien Levy Gallery Records, Julien Levy Papers, Philadelphia Museum of Art, Library and Archives.

Mina Loy Exhibition Catalogue

Mina Loy: Strangeness is Inevitable. Edited by Jennifer R. Gross. Princeton: Princeton University Press, 2023.

Mina Loy Biographies, Monographs, and Multi-Media Sources

Virginia M. Kouidis. *Mina Loy: American Modernist Poet*. Baton Rouge: Louisiana State University Press, 1980.

Carolyn Burke. *Becoming Modern: The Life of Mina Loy*. Berkeley: University of California Press, 1996.

Mina Loy: Woman and Poet. Edited by Maeera Shreiber and Keith Tuma. Orono: The National Poetry Foundation, 1998.

Alex Goody. *Modernist Articulations: A Cultural Study of Djuna Barnes, Mina Loy, and Gertrude Stein*. London: Palgrave Macmillan, 2007.

The Salt Companion to Mina Loy. Edited by Rachel Potter and Suzanne Hobson. Cambridge: Salt Publishing, 2010.

Lara Vetter. *Modernist Writings and Religio-Scientific Discourse: H.D., Loy, and Toomer*. New York: Palgrave Macmillan, 2010.

Jessica Burstein. *Cold Modernism: Literature, Fashion, Art*. University Park: Penn State University Press, 2012.

Sandeep Parmar. *Reading Mina Loy's Autobiographies: Myth of the Modern Woman*. London: Bloomsbury Academic, 2013.

Tara Prescott. *Poetic Salvage: Reading Mina Loy*. Lewisburg: Bucknell University Press, 2016.

Mina Loy: Navigating the Avant-Garde. Edited by Suzanne W. Churchill et al. Davidson College, 2017. mina-loy.com.

Sarah Hayden. *Curious Disciplines: Mina Loy and Avant-Garde Artisthood*. Albuquerque: University of Mexico Press, 2018.

Linda A. Kinnahan. *Mina Loy, Twentieth-Century Photography, and Contemporary Women Poets*. Abingdon: Routledge, 2019.

Laura Scuriatti. *Mina Loy's Critical Modernism*. Gainesville: University Press of Florida, 2019.

"Mina Loy, Paul Blackburn and Robert Vas Dias poetry reading," 1965. Special Collections & Archives, University of California San Diego, La Jolla, 2020. library.ucsd.edu/dc/object/bb32458123.

Mary Ann Caws. *Mina Loy: Apology of Genius*. London: Reaktion Books, 2022.

Yasna Bozhkova. *Between Worlds: Mina Loy's Aesthetic Itineraries*. Clemson: Clemson University Press, 2022.

Sara Crangle. *Elevated Realms: An Anatomy of Mina Loy*. Edinburgh: Edinburgh University Press, 2024.

Sara Crangle. *Nethered Regions: An Anatomy of Mina Loy*. Edinburgh: Edinburgh University Press, 2024.

Linda A. Kinnahan. *Feminist Modernism, Poetics, and the New Economy: Mina Loy, Lola Ridge, and Marianne Moore*. London: Routledge, 2025.

Acknowledgments

The stewardship of scholars, writers, editors, and curators has made it possible for Mina Loy and her dazzling creative output to be known. "Loy," in this volume, is a direct trace of this body of work. "Mina" lives between that body and my own.

Thank you to *Annulet* and *Lana Turner,* in which versions of some of these chapters appeared, and to Susquehanna University for supporting this project. Jennifer Ashby, thank you for identifying Evelyn Brent and for your contributions to the discourse around Loy. To Matvei Yankelevich, boundless gratitude for your belief in *Transcendental Factory,* for Winter Editions, and for the many ways you expand what is possible. To Alan Gilbert, thank you for your peerless editorial eye and for your love and generosity.

KARLA KELSEY is the author of six books, including the poetry collections *On Certainty* (Omnidawn) and *Blood Feather* (Tupelo), and the experimental essay *Of Sphere*, selected by Carla Harryman for the 2016 Essay Press Open Book Contest. A recipient of awards and fellowships from the Poetry Society of America, the Fulbright Scholars Program, and Yale University, she is the editor of *Lost Writings: Two Novels by Mina Loy* (Yale University Press) and the co-publisher of SplitLevel Texts.

Transcendental Factory: For Mina Loy
Copyright © Karla Kelsey, 2024

ISBN 978-1-959708-10-0
LCCN 9781959708100

First Edition, 2024 — 1200 copies

Winter Editions, Brooklyn, New York
wintereditions.net

The cover features a photograph of the American actress Evelyn Brent, circa 1920, photographer unknown.

WE books are typeset in Heldane, a renaissance-inspired serif designed by Kris Sowersby for Klim Type Foundry, and Zirkon, a contemporary gothic designed by Tobias Rechsteiner for Grilli Type. The layout and covers are done by the editor following a series design by Andrew Bourne. This book was printed and bound in Lithuania by BALTO print.

WE is grateful for the support of our subscribers, and extends special thanks to recent Supporting and Lifetime Subscribers: Anonymous, Anonymous (in memory of the Beaubiens), Yevgeniy Fiks, and Elizabeth T. Gray, Jr.

 Winter Editions

Emily Simon, IN MANY WAYS

Garth Graeper, THE SKY BROKE MORE

Robert Desnos, NIGHT OF LOVELESS NIGHTS, tr. Lewis Warsh

Richard Hell, WHAT JUST HAPPENED

Marina Tëmkina & Michel Gérard, BOYS FIGHT
[co-published with Alder & Frankia]

Claire DeVoogd, VIA

Monica McClure, THE GONE THING

Ahmad Almallah, BORDER WISDOM

Hélio Oiticica, SECRET POETICS, tr. Rebecca Kosick
[co-published with Soberscove Press]

Heimrad Bäcker, DOCUMENTARY POETRY, tr. Patrick Greaney

Robert Fitterman, CREVE COEUR

Karla Kelsey, TRANSCENDENTAL FACTORY: FOR MINA LOY

Alan Gilbert, THE EVERYDAY LIFE OF DESIGN

Betsy Fagin, FIRES SEEN FROM SPACE

Michael Kasper, START ANYWHERE

POSTCARDS FROM THE SIEGE, ed. Polina Barskova
[co-published with Blavatnik Archive]

Cristina Pérez Díaz, FROM THE FOUNDING OF THE COUNTRY

Sarah Riggs, LINES